One Day at a Time

And Other Stories

A. K. Frailey

Hardcover edition ISBN: 9798361472390

Website https://akfrailey.com/

Amazon Author Page
https://www.amazon.com/A.-K.-Frailey/e/B006WQTQCE

Cover Photo https://pixabay.com/photos/tree-sunset-clouds-sky-silhouette-736885/

A. K. Frailey Books

THE WRITINGS OF A. K. FRAILEY

Books for the Mind and Spirit

https://akfrailey.com/

Contemporary Literary Fiction

OLDTOWN Fly, Sparrow, Fly
OLDTOWN Brothers Born

Historical Science Fiction Novels

OldEarth ARAM Encounter
OldEarth Ishtar Encounter
OldEarth Neb Encounter
OldEarth Georgios Encounter
OldEarth Melchior Encounter

Science Fiction Novels

Homestead
Last of Her Kind
Newearth Justine Awakens
Newearth A Hero's Crime
Newearth Progeny
Newearth Relevance

Short Stories

It Might Have Been—And Other Short Stories 2nd Edition
One Day at a Time and Other Stories
Encounter Science Fiction Short Stories & Novella 2nd Edition

Inspirational Non-Fiction

My Road Goes Ever On—Spiritual Being, Human Journey 2nd Edition

My Road Goes Ever On—A Timeless Journey

The Road Goes Ever On—A Christian Journey Through The Lord of the Rings

Children's Book

The Adventures of Tally-Ho

Wise Home

Wise Home on Lily Pad Pond

Poetry

Hope's Embrace & Other Poems 2nd Edition

Table of Contents

Introduction

Some people have a "bucket list." They make plans to do important things before their earthly existence ends. They check off each activity as they get it done with the objective of having nothing left to do by the time they reach the grave.

Not me. I have a to-do list for the other side. And it gets longer all the time. I have a series of very important objectives once I reach the other side—hopefully the side where there's light to see by.

First, I want to be reunited with lost loved ones. Second, I'd really like to inhale the power of spell check, Grammarly, and all that science and algebra that confused the heck out of me as a kid. Third, I'd like to travel around the planet and visit all those interesting places I was way too tired to explore in my corporeal existence. Fourth, I want to meet the characters in my stories and novels.

Why not? I am sure that they exist somewhere. Perhaps on a planet in a neighboring universe? In the eternal time frame, my characters and I could settle down with a cup of tea and some chocolate chip cookies and seriously relax. Then we'd explore what happened after my curser stopped moving through their lives. Heaps of drama there, certainly.

The truth is, a good story never really stops living. The best compliment I ever received was from an editor who said that even after she finished my book, she couldn't stop thinking about the characters. They even followed her into the garden. High praise indeed. I'd like to take all the credit, but that wouldn't be fair. I may have come up with the ideas, but each character has his or her part to play, coming alive in ways I never imagined in the readers' minds.

Hopefully, my characters will be just as eager to meet me. After all, I'm Someone's character, and I hope to meet my Creator someday.

See, my list keeps growing. Just like my characters.

One Day at a Time

Originally published on The Writings of A. K. Frailey
8/27/2021

Sylvie loved to plan. So, when her mother's playgroup asked her to arrange the fun activities for the next academic year, she jumped at the chance and bought a huge poster board to outline the main events at their next meeting. When her husband pleaded with her to organize this year's work get-togethers, she grabbed her colored markers and fashioned a list of interesting icebreakers. The pièce de resistance was when her mom insisted that she contact all the family members about who would bring what for the Thanksgiving dinner. Finally! She could make sure that there were a variety of vegetables rather than an overabundance of mincemeat pies.

Monday and Tuesday were a blur of activity. Wednesday, she woke up to dark clouds on what should have been a bright, sunny day. She flipped the light bedsheet off her slim body and let it fall on her husband's prone form. Except, he wasn't there.

Fighting annoyance at these two contrary elements in her otherwise perfectly planned day, Sylvie leaped from her bed. And slipped on a sheen of water pooled before the French doors. Landing on her behind, she yelped in surprise. She stared at the open doors, the grey clouds still dribbling pathetic drops, and huffed. She was getting wet, and she didn't have time for that.

She climbed to her feet, one hand holding the bedpost, and murmured under her breath.

"Stupid weather report. It wasn't supposed to rain last night. I would've shut the doors."

A wail caught her attention. Baby Francie crying for breakfast, undoubtedly.

With a few alterations to her steps, she performed her daily ritual—slipped on her prearranged day clothes, changed the baby's diaper, dressed her in a cute summer outfit, and swung into the kitchen. She checked the daily menu. Ah, yes! Bran muffins with sliced bananas, juice, and black coffee for Dan. She frowned as she prepared the meal. Dan? Where was he? He had said something about a new exercise routine, but he should've told her when he was going to start. She had made exactly six muffins yesterday, and that meant he could have two for breakfast and take two for lunch, leaving just two for her and the baby. What was she going to do with four extra muffins?

The coffee maker spluttered and beeped—announcing in appliance talk— Mission Accomplished. Her stomach dropped at the sight of the half-full carafe. She hated the taste of coffee. Now it was going to go to waste. How terribly sad! If only Dan had informed her of his change of plans.

The rest of the morning went as scheduled, but when she pushed the cart down the shopping aisle, she was horrified to discover that all the Wednesday specials had been discontinued. Normally, she could find wonderful baked bread and dessert goodies at half price on the Wednesday-special cart, but it was nowhere to be seen. How disappointing! She almost asked the store manager but decided that she didn't want to seem like a complainer. She'd just have to wait till next week to have her sister over for tea and cake.

As rain poured from the sky, she rushed from the car with a bag of groceries and the baby clutched in her arms. She sped into her warm, stuffy house, fretting at the fact that the forecasters were really losing their touch. How could she plan any outdoor activities if they couldn't even warn her about a torrential storm?

Mechanically, she changed the baby into dry clothes, put the groceries away, checked the crockpot roast, and then sorted through her mail. No surprises there. Two bills and three advertisements.

One bill caught her eye. She frowned at it. It was due yesterday! How could they do that? Now she'd be hit with a late penalty! And she had itemized their billing down to the last penny.

Ugh! With the loss of the specials cart, the forecasters' failure, Dan's irresponsible communication skills, and now facing a late fee, she didn't know how she could suck up the courage to finish her planning schedule.

She plunked Francie into the playpen with freshly washed toys and labored to her bedroom. She tugged off her wet shirt and pants.

With robust steps, Dan entered the house, called out, "Hey, I'm home!" and then treaded across the living room floor.

Francie squealed.

Dan had surely swung her high into his arms.

Ignoring the fact that she'd have to wear the outfit she had planned to save for tomorrow's play-day gathering, she pulled on a clean shirt and pants and combed her hair. A glum face peered back at her from the mirror.

Dan sauntered in, both he and the baby smiling from ear to ear.

Irritated to the breaking point, Sylvie brushed past her husband and pounded into the kitchen. She'd put her perfect dinner on the table even though he certainly didn't deserve it.

Hot steam flushed her face when she swiped the cover off the crockpot.

Dan hustled in behind her. "What's wrong, honey?"

After sliding the roast onto a receiving platter, she ladled the potatoes and carrots into a bowl with precise motions. "It would be nice if you'd tell me of any change of plans. I try to run this house as well as I can, but I can't do anything right if you go around changing things without telling me." She placed the vegetable bowl in the center of the table and the meat platter to the left.

A perplexed frown etched its way across Dan's forehead. "What change of plans? I did everything pretty much the same as I always do."

Opening her eyes extra-wide, Sylvie decided to lure him in so he could see his mistake himself. *It's no good always making it easy on husbands. They never learn if you do that, heaven knows.* "What time did you go to work this morning?"

"The usual."

"Really? I made special muffins for us, and you weren't here to eat them." *There. Now he'll be sorry!*

"We have our board meeting at 6:30 on Tuesdays. Always have. You know that."

"But not on Wednesdays!" Ah, ha! She'd caught him now. He really should be ashamed.

Dan stared at his wife. Then he turned to his baby daughter. "Do you know what she's talking about?"

Francie drooled, grinned, and mashed syllables together into what could best be translated into "U-goo-ah-mmm-brp."

Steam blew out of Sylvie's ears.

Slapping his head, Dan jogged himself and baby out of the room, pounded up the stairs, tossed stuff around in her workroom, making Sylvie's eyes nearly pop from her head, and then plodded back downstairs.

She slapped napkins on the table like a general laying out his battle plans.

Dan tossed her color-coded calendar on the counter. "I knew it! And I was right." He nearly howled in laughter.

Francie wasn't sure she wanted to take matters that far. She offered a baby scowl to the world in general.

Tears welling in her eyes at the sacrilegious treatment of her plans, Sylvie sniffed back a choking sob. "How can you be so heartless? I worked hard on those plans, and you're treating them like a game. And it was you who missed my muffins!"

Instantly contrite, Dan wrapped one arm around his wife in a buck-up, you'll-make-it-through hug. "You marked Tuesday off the calendar. You never mark a day off until you go to bed."

A pathetic tear meandered down Sylvie's face. She swiped it away. No point in adding to her pain. “Of course, I did that last night. Why are you acting so devilishly mean?”

“What day does that make today?”

The image of a snake spitting venom filled Sylvie’s mind. She bit off the word. “Wednesday.”

Dan hugged her tighter. “No, honey. It’s Tuesday. Has been all day. You’ve been so busy, you packed two days into one.”

The thought that her husband was insane only bothered her a little less than the idea that he might be on to something. The world tilted. The universe expanded. Her baby burped. Then she met her husband’s eyes. And knew.

At the mom’s playday gathering, Sylvie treated the assembly to her color-coded chart and a dazzling array of baked specials from the Wednesday specials cart. Her husband’s co-workers patted Dan on the back for the best icebreakers they’d ever enjoyed at a work meeting. And Thanksgiving dinner was now well-planned and nutritionally balanced.

Only her husband and baby Francie knew that from that fateful Tuesday, despite Sylvie’s love of planning, she made sure that she lived only one day at a time.

Let Yourself Go

Originally published on The Writings of A. K. Frailey
9/10/2021

Rather not. Jeremiah slid into his seat at the back of the lecture hall and prayed that the scrawled message on the board referred to a campus cult's lack of original thinking rather than a preview of his professor's worldview.

A tall thin spectacle with a man-bun on top, a tie-dyed shirt, bloomers-like shorts, and flapping bedroom slippers sauntered up to the podium.

I should've taken the online class.

A young woman, mid-twenties, with long brown hair, wireframe glasses, and small build but toned legs dropped her bulging backpack by the third empty chair to the right of him.

But then again…

The room filled to capacity and Jeremiah opened his notebook, flipped it to a new section, and tapped his pencil.

The young woman slid a recorder to the front of her desk, then leaned back and closed her eyes.

What's this? A lazy beauty who gets through class by replaying the lecture when it suits her fancy?

Jeremiah shoved the thought—*Wish I'd thought of it*—far away. He rubbed his eyes. Between his mom's recent liver transplant, the store downsizing and leaving managers like him in the dust, and the new graduation regulations, he'd come to think that the universe was in a sour mood. He wasn't too sweet himself.

The professor started—digging into societal ills, cultural concerns, hot button issues, even picking on the front-row students like lab rats who couldn't escape the taunting labels expelled from his gut based on their hyperventilated one-word answers. "When you leave this class, you won't know yourself! Kiss mommy and daddy's straightjacket goodbye!"

Jeremiah dropped his head on his hands. "At least online I could've muted him."

"What? And missed all this fun?"

Jeremiah glanced over.

Beauty, still leaning back with her eyes closed, appeared very much asleep.

"Excuse me?"

The professor sucked in a lungful for another charge. "How can you say you know anything—you believe anything—until you've heard all sides? I'm here to bring you into direct contact with ALL SIDES!"

Beauty sat up, a frown making her nose wrinkle in an alarmingly adorable fashion. "He's a circle?"

The gut-busting laugh that exploded from Jeremiah made him clutch his notebook and pencil as he fled the room.

Two days later, Jeremiah hurried down the hall after his last class of the week. He had a ton of work over the weekend, his mom needed someone to fix her end table, which tended to send her books and medicines crashing to the floor by evening no matter how well she propped it up each morning, and he had an interview for a part-time manager position on Saturday. If he could finish the year with the stellar grades he started with, he'd be sure of a full-time position before the year was out.

Only one class stood in his way.

Beauty strode along with him into the library, her bulging backpack pressing her shoulders into a stooped position.

A million introductions flashed through his mind, creating a linguistic maelstrom, not unlike ancient Egyptian hieroglyphs on steroids. Lacking any rational brain cells to call upon, Jeremiah simply stepped in front of the pretty woman, halting her in her tracks.

She looked up and stared blankly.

Jeremiah tossed caution to the wind. "He's a circle?"

Astonishing how long she could maintain that blank expression.

He plowed on. "In class? The professor promised to bring us in contact with all sides..."

Comprehension filled her eyes. Light broke over the mountains. Beauty smiled. Then the gate slammed shut. "It's an English class! What's he doing—social engineering?"

The puppy inside every man has moments when he desperately wants to run around in wild circles with his tongue lolling out and a wide grin encompassing his face.

The library would not be the appropriate setting.

"You free? I'm about ready for a cup of—" He shrugged. "You name it, and I'll get one for you too."

She laughed.

Three hours later, Jeremiah took the steps to his parents' house two at a time. He stepped into the living room and caught his mom napping lopsided in a chair and his dad pacing in circles.

"Hey, Dad. Everything okay?"

His dad's tear-filled eyes glinted in the afternoon light. "She's slipping away, son. Won't be long now."

A day and a half later, Jeremiah finished the arrangements for his mom's funeral Mass and then ran as fast as his legs would carry him into class.

Well into the first hour, the professor was in his element, extolling the freedom of thought that would lead to well-formed lives and true humanity. With pounding steps, he labored across his personal stage, excoriating the fools who marched in lockstep with old traditions, unmindful of the variety of options available.

Beauty slouched in her seat, one hand covering her eyes.

Jeremiah slipped into his seat and, for the first time since his mom's death, felt the crushing loss that he knew he'd live with for the rest of his life. Only the words of scripture, the hymns, and songs, the candlelight comforted his aching soul. *May their souls and the souls of all the faithful departed, through the mercy of God...*

"Let go!" The professor hammered the podium like a preacher swearing hellfire to the damned.

"Where? You only offer a void." Beauty's face glowered, anger and hurt glaring through her eyes.

His chin up and hand raised, the professor demanded obedience. "Open your minds!"

So low—Jeremiah barely heard her words—Beauty's spirit screamed, "So, the wind can blow through?"

Snatching her hand, Jeremiah helped her grab her bag, and they hustled outside.

Beauty flopped against the wall. "I need that class. But I don't think I can stand his rants for another day."

Jeremiah nodded. "My mom just passed away. All I can think of is how much I wish I had her back—and he keeps screaming that I have to let go."

Beauty's eyes reflected from twin pools of grief. "I'm sorry."

Jeremiah sucked in a deep breath and took her hand. "Perhaps we should take his advice."

"Huh?"

"There are other classes." He shrugged. "It might mean summer school, but instead of this—"

"We can actually learn something." Beauty grinned. "We're more squares than circles, eh?"

His mom's endearing smile before his eyes, Jeremiah nodded, took Beauty's hand, and let go.

Welfare and Well-Being

Originally published on The Writings of A. K. Frailey 8/13/2021

David Koelth couldn't believe his luck. Even if it was well-earned. He deserved it, really. The award had his name on it, after all: *The Koelth Department of Welfare and Well-Being.*

David tossed the green apple left over from lunch into the air and caught it handily. He leaned back in his swivel chair before his Richman Hill Executive desk and surveyed his dingy office. Granted, he was on the top floor of the four-story building and had a decent view of the east side of town, but still, it was only a lecturer's office. An assistant had it before him, for Heaven's sake.

He glanced at his calendar marked in bold colors depicting the various hats he wore each day of the week. Educational Psychology Lecturer Mondays and Thursdays, Assistant Dean of the Health Department on Wednesdays and Fridays, published author working on his latest masterpiece—*Wholly You*—on Tuesdays (his favorite day of the week), and attentive husband and father Saturday and Sunday.

A yawn bubbled up from his middle. It was late on Friday afternoon, but he hadn't been able to get much done. Constant interruptions!

First, Mildred from accounting had taken issue with his taxes. Something about a form that no one told him to fill out and now "they had to take a tiny snippet"—her exact word choice—from his salary to make everything come out "even-steven" at the end of the year. What? Did the woman eat archaic expressions for breakfast? He'd give her a thesaurus for Christmas.

Then, Coach Max waddled in from the ballfield. How such an overweight guy managed his role as athletics director stumped David. Must have relatives in high places. *Or he knows where to get the choice meats and offers discounts for the university banquets.* The strange thing about Max was that he never really explained anything. He spoke in eyebrows and syllables.

Eyebrows in the up position. "Eh, you o-kay?"

David spent a half-hour of his very valuable time trying to figure out why Max had hefted his way to his office.

Turning beet red and sweeping the floor with his gaze, Max just leaned on the door frame and stared through those bulbous eyes with dreary pleading. For what... Only God and the next empty container of Dairy Queen chocolate chip ice cream would know for certain. He had tossed him his apple. Maybe the guy would get a clue.

Finally, just when he was putting the last touches on his monthly planner, his wife, Ruth, had phoned and insisted that the hot water heater was broken. Lord, have mercy. He had called the plumber three times this summer, and he sure as heck wasn't doing it again. He could shower at work while she figured out what she was doing wrong. No way in hell he'd fork out another hundred bucks for plungers, pipes, or screwed-up thermostats. Wait till the season got cold, then he'd think about it. Probably all in her head anyway.

Oh well, time to head to the club and see what was on tap. He didn't need a drink, but it'd be good to check on the guys and gals. Gossip was a university's lifeblood, and he had no intention of becoming anemic anytime soon.

~~~

Surprisingly, no one at the club seemed in the mood to chat. Not with him anyway. Had he forgotten to use deodorant this morning? He sniffed. Nope. Nothing wrong with him. Must be a full moon. Everyone was acting weird, like they had been having a con-fab when he arrived but wouldn't speak again till he left. He'd shrugged it off. If they wanted to get hot and bothered about sports' team failures, a roller-coaster economy, or the latest-greatest plan to serve the community, he was glad he'd missed it.

Apparently, there were no faculty leaks about his upcoming award. He had looked for silent congratulations or the ever-present green-eyed monster, but nothing of the sort. Just a few headshakes and shrugs.

Who cares about them?

He drove through snarly traffic in anticipation of his wife's Friday dinner special, his son, David Jr's, weekly school report, and his daughter, Lilly's, cuteness. He'd give David the pointers every high-school kid needed to be college-ready and enjoy the last days of Lilly's childhood since he knew perfectly well that once she became a teen, she'd become unbearable.
~~~

Inevitably, he'd have to distance himself so that she wouldn't use him as a cash box.

After arriving at his two-story colonial house with a wrap-around porch, he parked the car in the attached garage and sauntered into the house.

"Honey, I'm home!" He glanced around the quiet kitchen in the dim evening light. *What's going on? Where is everyone?*

He laid his leather briefcase on the counter and headed to the living room. His heart nearly stopped. Books and magazines lay scattered as if they'd left the room in a hurry.

What a mess! Is this what he'd worked all day to come home to?

David pulled out his phone, ready to give hell to his wife, then ordered pizza for dinner since clearly nothing would be ready in time for his growling stomach.

The doorbell rang.

Who the—? He charged forward, ready to dispatch the devil himself.

But he didn't need to. The devil already had plans.

~~~

David sat in the emergency room where his wife had just breathed her last, and the bodies of his children were stretched out nearby. The staff had brought them in so he could offer a personal goodbye.

He didn't have anything to offer. He couldn't think. Or feel.

A heavy tread paced forward.
~~~

David lifted his aching head and tried to make sense of what he was seeing.

Coach Max?

Max stopped before him and laid his meaty hand on David's shoulder. His voice shook with emotion. "So—so sorry."

That's all it took, and David lost all power of speech. For once he listened.

"We planned a big celebration for tonight—the guys from the department, Ruth, family and friends from all over were coming tonight. But Mildred—from accounting—fell and broke her wrist so she called Ruth. She and the kids hurried over to get the last details in place—except they never made it. A tired truck driver crossed the line. No one survived." His eyes welled in tears. "And this was supposed to be your glory day."

The Koelth Department of Welfare and Well-Being echoed in David's head like a devil's cackle.

—Five Years Later—

Dave closed his computer, leaned back in his office chair, and stared out the window, grateful for the view of the quiet neighborhood. *Friday again. I've got a lot to do.*

Footsteps padded closer. Max stuck his head in the doorway, tossed David a ripe red apple, and grinned. "I heard the news."

Catching the fruit with one hand, David smiled back at his friend. "No secret this time."

After losing sixty pounds, Max could saunter into the room. "You deserve it. I can't think of anyone else who has dedicated so much time and energy to others' welfare as you have these past few years."

David rose, grabbed his threadbare coat from the back of his chair and tucked the apple into the pocket. "What I should've been doing all along." He pointed to the door. "Want to meet at the track? I have a tutoring session at the community center in a couple of minutes, but I could meet you after that."

"Sure!" Max's grin widened, his eyes alight with happiness. "See what I mean; you're always helping people. You encouraged me to give up death burgers and get healthy. The department heads are finally doing the right thing—naming the department after you, a man of well-being if ever I knew one."

David patted Max on the shoulder as he headed for the door. "Thanks, my friend, but I had to refuse the honor."

Startled, Max blinked, his mouth dropping open.

"Don't feel bad. Maybe someday. But in the meantime," David opened the door and crossed over the threshold, "I went through too much hell to forget—it's best to wait till the fruit ripens to name the tree."

They Had Their Chance

Originally published on The Writings of A. K. Frailey
7/30/2021

Gianna sat in her living room before a shoebox filled with memories and stared at an old, taped-together letter. Anxiety scrambled after fear, chasing horror along the byways of her mind. How could he have done such a thing? But now she knew—for once and for all—she had done the right thing.

The screen door squeaked open. Her youngest, Janie, raced into the room, followed by her hyper-excited pup, tracking newly mown grass across the floor. "Mom! Guess what! There's a new cat in the neighborhood. It's black and white so I'm calling it Moonie."

After dropping the letter onto a stack of family photos, Gianna shoved the box into a wooden cabinet and shut the door. She prayed that she could do the same with the images filling her mind.

Pup raced around the room, dove onto the couch, and flopped down, her tongue lolling. Janie laughed and joined her partner in crime.

In perfect imitation of a miffed prison guard, Gianna crossed her arms, peered down at the two innocents, and growled, "Think you can wander in here carrying all outdoors with you, eh? Suppose you'll be expecting lunch, too, no doubt."

With some kind of child's extra-sensory perception, Janie scrunched her nose and tilted her head, listening for a hidden something.

Gianna relaxed her pose, returning to ordinary-mom.

Happy again, Janie tipped back her head and boldly proclaimed her really important news, "Dad says he wants grilled cheese, chips, and pickles for lunch."

Gianna rolled her eyes and headed for the kitchen, glad for the distraction. "Oh, yeah? He wants *your* favorite lunch?" She hunched her shoulders in dejection. "And here I planned on liver and gizzards with a side dish of boiled onions. Oh, gee. I never get what I want."

Janie and her sidekick bounced off the couch and followed in close proximity, perhaps to make double-sure that mom hadn't gone to the dark side. She even scooted to the refrigerator and yanked out the cheese package just to be safe.

The puppy lapped up a bowl of water, while Janie propped her head on her hands, sitting at the kitchen counter, her eyes following her mom's every move.

Pushing every thought away, except how to make extra-good grilled cheese sandwiches, Gianna performed mom-magic and prepared a delicious, healthy lunch just in time for her husband to tromp in, stomping a pile of cut grass and weeds on the doormat.

Matt looked up sheepishly. "Sorry, but I had to do a lot of cutting, or we'd need a compass and a map to get through the backyard."

A waterfall of gratitude sluiced Gianna from head to foot. She could barely get out her words. "Thanks, sweetheart."

With a perplexed frown, Matt peeled off his shoes, padded in his grungy socks across the room, eyed the lunch spread, and shot a high-five to his daughter.

Janie giggled.

Pup slept curled up in her corner. A perfect picture of creature comfort.

Gianna sat next to her husband, and they clasped hands as they said grace over the meal, their heads bowed. Then everyone dug in, filling their plates. Suddenly, the image of the torn and taped letter flooded Gianna's mind. Choking back a sob, she ran out of the room.

~~~

The July sun finally released the day, and dark coolness settled over the bedroom as Gianna readied for bed.

Matt hadn't said anything since she had told him to leave her in peace for a bit. She had cried for over an hour, and her eyes were still puffy at dinner time.

Matt had taken Janie to his parents' house where they fed the assortment of dogs, cats, and hummingbirds awaiting their return from Mount Rushmore. He had simply offered a quick kiss on Gianna's cheek and roared off with a squealing-happy Janie down the road.

Thank God.

Alone in the house, Gianna pulled out the old shoebox and tipped it upside down. She spread out the photographs, putting them into chronological order: her parents' wedding photo, her brother's fifth birthday party, Thanksgiving with Grandmother and Papa, her sister's third birthday party, Christmas with Aunt Selina. Her
~~~

baptism. Everyone had looked so happy, smiling so brightly for the camera.

There were no photos of the fights, the drunken spells, the rampages. No copy of the divorce decree. Only the one letter. Torn into pieces. It had been taped so that the edges matched, and the words, though dim, were clear enough to read.

"I love you..."

Gianna plunked down on the edge of her bed, her gaze straying to the fireflies sparkling just outside the window.

Matt padded in and sat down next to her, their shoulders touching. "You ready yet?"

She nodded, tears filling her raw eyes again. "He loved her. He really did. And I never knew."

"This has to do with that box you found at your mom's, doesn't it?"

She nodded. "All the old photos and a love letter—from Dad to Mom."

Matt didn't shrug or murmur. He just clasped his hands, his head bowed, listening.

"I never knew them as a happy couple. I only knew the fights and all the nasty stories they told about each other. When Dad died, mom seemed relieved. She never once said a kind word about him. When she died, I only grieved for what I'd never known."

Matt cleared his throat, pausing, parsing his words carefully. "It bothers you that he once loved her? That they loved each other—long ago? Like maybe that'll happen to us?"

Gianna glanced over and saw a wrinkle of concern on her husband's forehead. "No. Not that. I understand that what tore them apart is on them. It's not us." She sniffed back her pain and straightened. "No, what got me was that despite everything, I still believed in marriage. I dared to hope." She took her husband's hand and caressed the ring on his finger. "By some miracle, we did what they couldn't."

Matt nodded and clasped her hand in his. "Or wouldn't." He stood and led her to the bed, pulling the soft sheet back and letting her slide under the coolness. He leaned over and wiped away the last vestige of a tear. "What'll you do with the letter?"

She sighed as she leaned back on the pillow, expectantly awaiting her husband at her side. "I'll put it away. After all, they had their chance."

Matt climbed into bed and wrapped his arms around her.

Gianna snuggled in close. "Now it's my turn."

I'm Making Mine

Originally published on The Writings of A. K. Frailey
7/16/2021

Imogen trudged down the porch steps of her sister's farmhouse, doing a quick kindness and her civic duty. She crossed the yard, lugging two large bags to the burn barrel while pattering footsteps followed close behind. She hoped it wasn't the murdering demon that had kept her up half the night, sending some unknown critter to its untimely end.

"Hey, auntie, let me help you with that."

Without so much as a by-your-leave or an explanation that the trash bag was white and the Goodwill bag was black, Lucy flung the two bags over the edge of the canister, where they landed with a definite thud.

Lucy, medium height, dyed jet-black hair, pale skin, and wearing a man's tank top over artistically torn shorts, clapped imaginary dirt off her grubby sixteen-year-old hands and grinned. "I have something important to tell you."

Tugging the black bag back out of the barrel, Imogen grunted her version of well-get-it-over-with.

Her posture decidedly more formal, hands-on-hips, shoulders back, and her eyebrows bunched, Lucy launched her declaration like a night missile into rebel territory. "I'm going evil. Really bad. It's a choice, and I'm making mine."

Maxwell Smart's voiceover played in Imogen's head, "...for niceness instead of evil." She flung the salvaged bag over her shoulder and tromped across the wet grass, her damp shoes sliding with each step.

Lucy pranced alongside, wringing her hands into unnatural whiteness. "Didn't you hear me?"

Imogen stopped at her car door and dropped the bag on the gravel driveway. "I'm doing my absolute best to ignore you. Now, go inside to your mother and break her heart—after every good thing she's done for you. I have to drop this off at Goodwill before they close, or I'll be stuck driving it to Mass in the morning with Old Man Davy and his wife pretending they don't notice a thing."

"Would it bother them so much if you have an old bag in your car?"

"They wouldn't care, really. But they'll have nothing to talk about, so they'd ask. And then I'd have to explain that I stopped by my sister's place yesterday, being today, and it would slip out that my niece tried to burn the blinking thing before I could get it to Goodwill."

A microcosm of a grin twitched over Lucy's face. "So, you wouldn't tell them that I've gone evil?"

"You tried to burn a donation to charity. Enough said, honey."

A prolonged sigh followed Lucy as she directed her feet to the porch steps. "No one understands me."

Least of all you, child. Imogen swung the bag into the back seat and plunked her body before the steering wheel. She drove down the lane at the moderately safe speed of forty miles per hour.

~~~
~~~

Pulling into her driveway, Chancy, Imogen's Irish Setter and sorry excuse for house security, bounded forward. What does one say to a happy-go-lucky dog? What she always said, "Yes, I love you, but don't jump. It's bad manners."

Ignoring not only manners but decency itself, Chancy scrabbled forward and propped her muddy paws on Imogen's clean pants.

"Glad I already made my Goodwill run. They'd have offered *me* clothes if I'd arrived like this." She blew a stray lock of hair from her face and stepped around three cats prancing in her path.

In the kitchen, she surveyed the wreckage. Though it happened every time she left the house, it always took her by surprise. The fresh mess. And, of course, neither Carl nor the kids would know how it happened. Bread crumbs, a jelly smear, a dollop of peanut butter, a couple of stray raisins and a banana peel informed her of recent culinary adventures. Brad, undoubtedly. The boy was growing faster than poison ivy around the utility pole. Not his fault. Nor his dad's. *Not mine either, come to think of it.* She shook her head. *But your mom has a lot to answer for.*

Her sixty-five-year-old husband, with a hint of arthritis in his joints, lumbered into the room. A good twenty pounds overweight and sporting the unshaved look, Carl swallowed the last of what smelled like the missing banana and offered a half-wave. "Jane high-tailed it to work an hour late, and Joe's gone off with friends to a game. Had to eat early. So, I made sure he got some fruits and vegetables."

Imogene wrung out a wet dishcloth and rounded up the crumbs. "How's that?"

"I made him add raisins and corn chips to his PBJ."

She brushed the crumbs into the trash and started on the dirty dishes. "Why would he agree to do that? Sounds terrible."

"He wanted twenty bucks. Nothing's for free in this world." Carl leaned against the counter and appeared to mull over the ponderous truth he'd just revealed to the world.

Imogene wiped her hands on a dry towel and stared fixedly at her husband. "You bribed your grandson to eat our good food with your hard-earned money?"

Carl let that sink in. "Yep. That's about the size of it." He patted her shoulder. "But I've been busier than a bee in springtime. Got that raccoon carcass buried past the fence line, fixed the wobbly back step, and put a chuck roast in a pan with garlic, onions, carrots, and some of our new potatoes."

Pride shining through his eyes, he opened the oven door. "Just waited till you got home to turn it on. Shouldn't take long."

Pleased but stuck on the words "raccoon carcass," Imogene flashed a falling-star smile. "What'd you bury?" She tilted her head to the left. Her hearing had never been good, but after today, she seriously debated the benefits of a hearing aide.

"You know, the coon that lost the big battle last night?"

"I heard the battle; I just didn't know who the participants were. Or who won."

"Didn't see any winner badges. Just the loser stiff as a board in the garage this morning. Though, he was laid out near Chancy's food bag."

"Chancy has never killed anything in her life. Too silly."

Carl shrugged. "Everyone has their limits. Guess old coon pushed them too far."

Imogene planted a kiss on her husband's cheek, pressed the bake button until it read 400, and then started toward her bedroom. "I'm going to change out of these clothes and lay down a moment." She stopped and glanced over her shoulder. "Lucy told me that she's going evil now. Picked out clothes to match and everything."

Carl snorted. "Yeah. Good luck with that."

Imogene turned around and propped her hand on the counter. "She said it was her choice." Shaking her head, she tried to toss Lucy's baby picture out of her mind. "We never considered that option."

Carl started for the backdoor. "Oh, yes, we did. Just didn't tell anyone. Not like kids today. Good Lord, they tell everyone everything."

"And why is that?"

"Don't know, honey." Carl passed through the doorway and creaked down the back steps.

Later that night as she lay in bed, Imogene had to give it to her husband. Her belly felt as satisfied with dinner as it had ever been. She enjoyed resting comfortably in her husband's embrace. Sometimes his ways sent shivers of irritation through her whole body, but right now, perfect calm flooded her being. The soft feel of his arms around her middle, fitting together as perfectly as spoons in the kitchen drawer.

After a day of small duties where challenges rose from the murky depths of thoughtless minds, she closed her eyes and settled her heart to the drumroll of raindrops against the window pane. No murdering demons tonight.

We Get Along

Originally published on The Writings of A. K. Frailey
7/2/2021

Weary after a long day at work, Everleigh forced down a tuna salad at the kitchen counter as evening closed in. Blessedly, a cool wind rippled the curtains, relieving the furnace-blast heat of the hot summer day. Body and soul still together, she patted her sleepy do-nothing cat as it dozed on the couch and then padded down the white hallway to her bedroom.

Her phone binged, notifying her that she had received a message. Without even looking at it, she placed it by her bedside and began her evening routine. A cold shower would revitalize her, surely.

Well, that didn't work.

Bleary-eyed, she brushed her teeth and then plopped onto her bed.

Boring rote days, toss-and-turn nights, and high humidity drained her will to live.

She stared at the fan. "Don't just hang there."

Stepping to the wall switch, she did the needful and then grabbed her phone on the way back to her bed.

"Dad?" She scrolled to the message.

Your grandpa is arriving on Sunday to celebrate his 90th.

Hope you'll come too.

Love, Dad

The scene from *The Lord of the Rings* where Frodo sets off from Rivendell, heading to Mount Doom in order to save the Shire, flashed through her mind.

It's not quite that bad.

Ignoring the jittery goosebumps that raced up her arms, she scrolled down.

Yep. There's the address. "Dad doesn't miss a beat."

With a mighty effort, she gripped her will by the collar. *Behave yourself!* She talked out loud to encourage her flagging spirits. "Dad never asks for much, and he hasn't seen grandpa in years. I'll be merciful and go along."

She squinted as she googled the address.

"Oh, wait! That's way south. Nearly in another state. There's no direct road!"

Panic reared its ugly head, and Everleigh sucked in a shuddering breath. Then her phone binged again.

What now? The whole thing's been canceled? Sure, that's it. Thank you, God. I promise I'll—

The thought—*Check the message before making any promises*—wiggled through her brain.

She scrolled down.

Aunt Kate needs a ride. Pick her up on the way, okay?

No "please, dear daughter." Not even an emoji grimace—a way of saying, "Sorry for the horrific situation I'm putting you in."

Her fingers itched to tap back a formal message stating, "Everleigh died last year and was peacefully buried in the local cemetery." She'd even be willing to pay for a tombstone to make it look good.

Dying was one thing. Being buried under her family's strange coping mechanisms was quite another.

~~~

The thing about Aunt Kate, Everleigh reminded herself as she sped along the country road, was that she had lost the ability to communicate decades ago, but no one had the heart to tell her.

She parked her car in front of the tiny white ranch house in the quiet neighborhood and peered in the back seat, mentally reviewing her to-do list. Blanket for Auntie—since ninety-five degrees in the shade just won't cut it for her old bones. A bottle of cola, two root beers, a water bottle, and a flask of gin. She'd make her way through them with unerring determination. Heaven help her if she forgot one of the nectars of the gods.

Her sainted sister, Jane, would take care of the food. Jane would also take care of the decorations, insurance policies, and would make sure that two televisions were blaring—one covering the conservative side of world affairs, the other keeping the liberals in touch with hot-button issues. Of course, the internet would be available at all times.

Or the universe would evaporate.

Ready to leap forth and assist her eighty-something aunt, Everleigh froze when the old woman speed-hobbled down the walk swinging her cane. "Open the door, honey cakes! Can't ya see I'm ready?"

According to Google maps, the drive was only supposed to take two and a half hours. According to Everleigh's comfort barometer, the drive was interminable.
~~~

The old woman chatted rapid-fire for several minutes, then asked incomprehensible questions.

Repeat.

After using every stock answer in the omniverse, Everleigh soon reverted to "Hmmm" and "you don't say?"

Aunt Kate was not amused.

~~~

Everleigh's dad, on the other hand, seemed to find everything and everyone funny. He never laughed out loud, just let the glitter in his eyes chuckle at the cymbal-clash reality of the family gathering.

Out back, her brother-in-law-number-two, Donnie, barbecued ribs and turkey burgers for those who either wanted delicious food or clean arteries. Jane sent the vegans into ecstasy with crispy buffalo cauliflower bites, oil-free pumpkin pancakes made with gluten-free flour, and no-tuna salad sandwiches.

The two teens in attendance peeled off into opposite corners of the house and played multiplayer games with people on the other side of the globe.

Grandpa sat stage center stretched out on a lawn chair, a mild afternoon sun brightening his pale face. His wandering wide-eyed gaze reflected little of his glory years serving in two wars and then managing a realty business for forty years, till grandma died and all her money sense was buried with her.
~~~

After seeing that auntie was stashed safely at the picnic table where she could snatch whatever food or drink took her fancy, Everleigh wandered about, checking to see if there were any friendly aliens about the place.

Naw. Just family.

Then a hand tapped her shoulder and Everleigh shrieked. She turned and stared into the blackest eyes she had ever seen. Set in a golden face crowned with blue-black shiny hair that trailed down a straight back, Everleigh realized that beauty knew how to arrange her jewels.

The woman thrust out a hand. “Sorry, didn’t mean to scare you. Just wanted to introduce myself. I’m Lekha, a nursing student from the hospital where your sister works. I watch over your grandpa whenever she’s too busy or something special is going on.”

Everleigh shook the offered hand and tried to think of coherent words. “Oh?” *Where was Auntie’s quick wit now?* “Well, that’s good of you. To come all this way—” She glanced over her shoulder.

Jane’s boy, Earl, sat beside the old man, showing him something on his phone. *A game, probably.*

Unabashed, Lekha took in the scene with an expression suggesting that not only was her eye color different, her vision was too. “I enjoy it. Seeing a family together is refreshing, lifts my spirits.”

Everleigh gawked. She clamped her mouth shut to keep it from dropping open. She swept her gaze over the yard. Probably fifteen people in all and no large family confabs. All intimate clusters. Each to their own niche.

"We're not a very cohesive group, I'm afraid. We get along by not having too much to do with each other."

Lekha grinned. "Most of my family is home in India. I'm here studying. At least your family is on the same continent. That's something."

Earl stepped up, barging into the conversation as entitled people often do. He beckoned Lekha with a waving hand. "Hey, you gotta come and check on grandpa. I think he's thirsty, but he's trying to drink the hand sanitizer."

Undisturbed by this newest proof of borderline insanity, Lekha hurried away to her duty.

Everleigh strolled over to her dad, who stood near the empty grill holding a sampler plate—a bit of everything on there. "You having a good time?"

He shrugged. "I don't come to have a good time."

Everleigh sighed. "I thought that was the point."

Her father took a bite of a buffalo cauliflower and shook his head. "Honey, we can't make each other happy. But we can get along well enough to celebrate a person's life while he's still with us. That's pretty good, in my book." He lifted a pumpkin pancake and offered it to her.

Hungry for the first time in days, Everleigh took a bite.

He'd Be There, Waiting

Originally published on The Writings of A. K. Frailey
6/18/2021

Clouds covered the sun, breaking the intense heat of the evening, as Sonia climbed the last of the steep steps, trudged across her porch, and, juggling her bag of groceries, swung open the kitchen door. "Lord, it's too hot for June. Can't we save this till July? I can't take it."

The front entryway didn't respond. Though Delmar, her German Shepard, started barking from the backyard.

She plopped the shopping bag on the counter, shoved her personal bag, which, if one looked closely, resembled her college backpack, off her shoulder, and stomped to the back door. She twisted the handle and yanked.

Delmar sped into the house like a red Mercedes in the right lane.

Falling backward on impact, she smashed her hand against the counter and swore at the devoted animal. "Dammit, Dog, you know better. Trying to kill me? The one who feeds you?"

Contrite, Delmar whined and attempted a sloppy make-up kiss.

Sonia wasn't in the mood. Amazed at herself, she realized that she wanted to smack the dog. *What's wrong with me?*

Not getting anywhere in the reconciliation department, Delma trotted to the metal dishes set beside the refrigerator and inhaled a bowl of tepid water. Next, he crunched the last remaining bits of breakfast, nosing the bowl across the room in the process.

Normally, the dog's self-involved obsession would set her laughing. But not today.

Her stomach grumbled. The workplace café had undergone new management, and without a sane thought to their long-range business, they decided to hike the daily lunch prices to nearly twice their usual. In protest, and because she honestly couldn't afford them, Sonia swore off their offerings until they came to their senses.

But that left her no reasonable options at noon. And it was after six now.

She filled a pot with water and set it to boil, then pulled the pasta box from her bag. She lined up all the ingredients for a healthy spaghetti supper: whole tomatoes, onions, peppers, lean ground beef, and a jar of spicy sauce. She even rooted through the highest shelf above the stove, the one where she hid the tempting stuff—chocolate chip cookies and red wine.

She'd make a night of it. Long, impossible days deserved a reward, right?

Something was off with her logic, but she shook her head and pulled the wrapping off the meat, then set it to sizzle in the frying pan. Next, she set the chopping board on the counter, and she was on her way. Oh, the wine! She poured a healthy glass, lifted it to her lips, and—

The doorbell buzzed, sending her nerves into fits.

Delmar went into full-frenzy mode. As far as he was concerned, aliens might have landed their spaceship at the door.

A headache sprouting behind her eyes, Sonia took a sip and trotted to the front room. Yanking the dog back, she took a quick look out the window.

Awe, dang it! Jim and Eva. Grinning like fools.

They saw her, and their hesitant smiles ballooned outlandishly.

Mumbling under her breath, she informed her dog of the real state of her mind. "I thought when I moved in this neighborhood, I'd finally be free of—"

Whining, Delmar looked scandalized. He scratched at the door. Company was waiting!

In defeat, she opened the door.

"Hi!" Twin voices, Jim's baritone and Eva's soprano, melded in perfect harmony.

What? They practice on the sly?

Her weak response didn't hinder them from barging right in, their happiness bouncing along with them.

Eva gushed, "We saw you drive up and waited, but we couldn't stand it any longer. We just had to stop by and share the news!"

Sonia forced a smile. They were already married, so what…?

Eva's slim hand caressed her belly.

"We're expecting!" The two voices harmonized like a well-practiced song.

Forcing a return smile, Sonia itched to slap someone. Instead, she gushed back. "Oh, how wonderful! So happy for you. Great news." She swallowed the bile rising in her throat and waved toward the kitchen. I was just giving myself a little reward after a hard day. Want to join me?"

No second invitations needed. The two lovebirds pranced into the kitchen, Eva leading and patting a remarkably sedate dog on the head.

Delmar let them pass like the gentleman he never was.

Sonia sneered. “He usually jumps all over people.”

Eva rubbed the dog under the chin. “Oh, we’re good friends. I see him out in the yard during the day; he seems lonely, so when I have a moment, I call him over, and we have a good chat.” She grinned at the canine. “You’re a great listener, aren’t you, Buddy.”

After mouthing “traitor” at the dog, Sonia pulled two glasses from the shelf and started to pour.

Eva backed off with a look of horror. “Oh, no, not me.” She rubbed her mid-section. “Can’t take a chance with the baby.”

Jim rubbed his wife’s back, his gaze dropping to the floor.

What’s he looking so sheepish about? Going to melt into a puddle all over my clean floor.

Holding herself together with superwoman grit and the better part of the wine and cookie supply, Sonia listened to their happy plans for as long as she could stand it. Then she yawned and exclaimed over the late hour. “I’ve got to get up early tomorrow...”

With a blushing retreat, the blessed couple found their way home.

Sighing in relief, Sonia toddled off to bed. The ingredients of her spaghetti dinner were all but forgotten on the counter.

~~~

Grateful for the respite on a cloudy, low 80s, August day, Sonia lugged her latest dinner ingredients into the house and onto her counter.

A techno-snafu had shut the office down early, so she made it home before the clock struck noon. She hummed in the quiet kitchen, enjoying the peaceful opportunity. Then she looked up and frowned. Not a sound from Delmar. *Where is that dog?*

She unlocked the back door and swept her gaze across the backyard. Nothing. Fear clutched her chest.

Then a flash of red caught her eye. There in the back corner, Delmar sat on his haunches while a woman crouched on the other side of the chain-link fence and reached through, patting his smooth fur. *Who the—?* Sonia squinted and recognition settled her heart to a normal rhythm.

She sauntered over. In a joking tone, she called out, "He's spoiled enough. He'll want his meals on golden dishes next."

Eva glanced up; her face blotched, almost as red as her shirt. She snatched her hand back.

Sonia stumbled. "Oh—hey, just joking. Go ahead and pet him. He's alone a lot. Loves company."

With a nod, Eva reached out and stroked the dog's ears.

Delmar grinned in doggy ecstasy.

Tiny alarm bells ringing, Sonia dragged her memory back to the last time she'd seen Eva. Months ago. When she and Jim came by with the great news. Her stomach clenched at the memory.
~~~

She steeled herself. *Oh, what the heck.* "So, how're you doing?" She tilted her head, trying to see. *No baby bump yet, that's for sure.*

Swallowing convulsively, Eva's hand shook even as it went limp.

Delmar seemed to understand. He pushed his face against the mesh and tried to lick his neighbor's face.

A tiny bubble of laughter (or was it despair?) burbled to the surface. Eva choked.

The alarm bells went from tinkles to gongs, pealing their warning. Sonia crouched closer. "Sorry. I didn't mean—"

Eva pulled her hands onto her lap. "I'm not so good. We lost the baby."

Sonia sucked in a pain-filled breath. "I-I'm sorry." What else could she say?

"So are we. Can't always get what you want."

Best foot forward, Sonia chose the encouraging, supportive path. "You can always try again."

The woman's convulsive swallow turned into a sob. "We did. Lost 'em both."

"Oh, God."

A meek nod. Eva climbed wearily to her feet. She stared at Delmar. "He's a good listener."

Sonia waited.

Eva finally met her gaze. "I really wanted this baby." Pain shared. She turned and slogged to her house.

Sonia stood stunned as realization hit her. Their pain was much the same.

Delmar whined and nudged her hand with his wet nose.

Sonia peered down.

The clouds parted, and the hot August sun baked her shoulders. All hope of dinner evaporated.

~~~

When the doorbell buzzed at sundown, Sonia wasn't surprised to see Jim's face staring back at her from the porch window. She let him in without comment.

He paced to the far side of the living room and turned.

Delmar plopped down in the corner with a decided harumph. Clearly, he knew he was not the center of attention.

Sonia pointed to the kitchen. "Can I get you something?"

His face drawn and lined with grief, Jim shook his head. "Thanks. We ate earlier. I just came by to thank you."

Startled, Sonia narrowed her gaze. Was he joking? A passive-aggressive thing?

Jim stepped closer, inviting a moment of intimate conversation. "No one understands. Just because the baby was so young, some people think that it didn't matter. It wasn't real. My aunt even teased us about having a burial. Said it was like burying a foot after an amputation. Or a lost tooth."

Rage writhed inside Sonia, a beast she corralled almost every day of her adult life. "That's stupid."

Jim nodded. "Cold, really. But you understand. And Eva needed to be heard. So, I just wanted to thank you."
~~~

Flummoxed, Sonia fought impending tears. "*I* didn't do anything." Slashing against scars that had nearly ruined her life, she snipped her words into tiny pieces. "I don't know what you're talking about."

Jim's eyes widened, clearly shocked. "Oh, sorry, Eva thought that you'd lost a baby too. That you understood her pain."

"I never told her that!" Sonia was surprised by her scream. Guttural, ripping her insides out.

Wordlessly, Jim shook his head. His expression spoke for him. *You never lost a baby?*

"I can't lose something I never wanted—never admitted!"

Crushed, Jim's face fell into a chasm of grief. "Oh, yes. You can." He strode across the room, swung open the door, glanced from Delmar to Sonia's face, then plunged outside and plummeted down the steps.

Sonia fell to her knees, a sob taking her places she had refused to go for years.

Delmar inched closer and nudged his head under her arm. At some point, she would stop crying, and he'd be there, waiting for her.

For That, I was Glad

Originally published on The Writings of A. K. Frailey
6/4/2021

Balloons have no business on the ground. It's quite obvious why, and I shouldn't have had to explain it to anyone, much less my nearest and dearest. But then, one has to explain everything these days, doesn't one?

I had just lost a tooth. One I had been particularly fond of as it made chewing so much easier. It was a chilly spring afternoon, and I was at the college graduation party for my niece, Marley-May. A child saddled with such a legal title deserved my compassion, as well as monetary encouragement, so I generously supported my favorite niece through five years of college. It took her a year and a half to change her major six times. But once she settled on Art Therapy with a minor in Anxious Languages taught by a guy named Phil-something, she plowed right through.

Using every ounce of her hard-earned sensibility, Marley-May was dressed for the weather that morning in a skin-tight, sleeveless dress and high heels. The spring thunderstorm held off until the last of the graduates made it across the stage. Then it swooped in for revenge.

I and sundry family, faculty, and community members scattered to our cars and made it to graduation ceremonies throughout town, gripping steering wheels and squinting into failing light.

My sister, Marley-May's mom, Geraldine, had decorated the garage with streamers, balloons, and hung a huge, stenciled swag: CONGRATULATIONS, NOW GET A JOB!

Piled high with sandwiches, snacks, cakes, and drinks of all kinds, a standard plastic table dominated the oil-stained, cement floor. An array of nails and screws piled up in old tin cans lining the shelving was a sight to behold. I had no idea that Geraldine's husband, Sherman, was into recycling. I admired his organizational skills almost as much as I admired Geraldine's damn-the-torpedoes approach to life's challenges. Her husband's projects among them.

Then, I took a bite of a caramel candy and promptly broke my tooth. But I couldn't tell *her* that. So, I wrapped the piece in a matching "Congratulations, Now Get a Job" napkin and grinned through my discomfort.

"Having a good time?"

I glanced at my sister and grimaced. "Course. I love these get-togethers."

She grimaced back. "Liar."

"You know me too well."

"I know that you made this day possible. Marley's got a lead on a job, and her future looks bright. Thanks to you."

I lifted my gaze beyond Geraldine's left shoulder and watched my happy niece swigging back a soda with a half-eaten sandwich in the other hand. She chattered excitedly in a gathering of two other gals and a couple of interested, though not overly enthusiastic, young men. Did she have any idea how harsh the world would be? How dreams would be dashed? Aspirations squashed? The mighty burden of reality overload?

I shook my head. Of course not. She wouldn't be smiling right now if she knew. Like a young bride going on her honeymoon, there's no warning in the world to prepare a person for real sacrifice. That few care to notice. Even when it costs everything.

Geraldine patted my hand.

I met her gaze.

"You've done more than your fair share."

"I did what needed to be done. Like what you did for Mom."

"I just read her stories and relived my childhood as she slept in a chair."

"You also held her hand. That's what mattered."

Geraldine's eyes filled with tears.

Sherman marched into the make-shift party grounds and boomed. "Hey, I got old family videos set up in the living room and there's hot cocoa on the stove. Let's take this party to new heights, shall we?"

Wide-eyed horror rippled over Marley's face.

Geraldine stood and faced the crises with charming calm. "Family videos are for us older folks who have no plans tonight." She sidled into the youth's gathering and drew her daughter aside. They spoke, and Marley looked over.

My stomach sank. The obligatory thank you was heading my way, complete with the hunted look and swift backward glances, pleading for courage from her friends.

Marley stopped in front of me and wrung her hands, her shoulders thrust back, ready to do her duty. "Hey, Auntie, just wanted to thank you for everything. I never could have made it through college without your support."

I nodded graciously. The sharp edge of my tooth cut my tongue. "Happy to help. 'What good you can do, you should do,' Mom always said." I shrugged. "Besides, Joe left me more than I really needed. It was only right that I share."

A perplexed expression squinted through Marley's eyes. "Oh, the money was nice. But what I really mean was your—I don't know—your being you. Always there. Someone who cared about *me*." She glanced over her shoulder. "Mom and dad are great. But, you know, they don't always understand."

The combination of honest flattery and dishonest betrayal sliced through me.

Words fell from my lips before I could stop them. "No one understands us completely, Honey. Only bits and pieces. The parts that reflect what we know. The rest confuses the hell out of us. We just try not to get mean about it."

A startled glimmer of understanding quivered over Marley's face.

Then a high, laughing voice rose from the background, "Hey, Graduate, you coming?" One of the gals pointedly tapped her watch. Fun called. Best not be late.

Marley squeezed my hand and smiled, peering into my eyes as if to convey something no words could tell. *Real gratitude?*

I nodded in acceptance and let her go her way.

Geraldine swept the remnant of the party-goers inside while Sherman took charge of clearing the faded festive grounds.

I stood and swiped my wrapped tooth from beside my paper plate. *I'll get it fixed next week. Geraldine will fill me in on Sherman's newest home-improvement project, and Marly will find a job, making a life somewhere, somehow.*

A red balloon skittered out of my way as I stepped across the floor. I picked it up and carried it with me. For a while, at least, it could hang in honor on my kitchen wall.

And for that, I was glad.

Library

Originally published on The Writings of A. K. Frailey
5/21/2021

Robert sat back on the wooden library chair, pushed an award-winning thriller aside and stared down the packed double rows of books. Heavy weighted shelves topped with hardcover novels that couldn't fit in their appointed place lined the room. An oversized GREEK MYTHS illustrated cover stared at him from a shelf mounted on a pillar directly ahead. The back wall, plastered with paperback mysteries and romances, while the front entrance, dominated by newspapers and magazines, offered a neat but plentiful aura to the room. A wooden rack sported an array of local t-shirts for sale, and community news splashed itself over a mounted bulletin board.

He chuckled. History behind, romance to the left, political figures to the right. Myths and legends directly ahead. *I should be well-educated or happily entertained, at least.*

The heavy oak front door creaked as a patron entered. A middle-aged woman dressed in a sweatshirt and jeans bearing an armload of books lumbered to the front desk.

The librarian, an older woman with white hair and thin glasses, glanced up. She smiled in welcome.

Robert frowned. *She didn't smile when I entered.*

A muted conversation ensued.

He really should pick out a couple of books, or get back to work, or deal with Beatrice's issues...but the voices oozed with understanding friendship.

"You liked it?"

"Oh, yeah. Reminded me of the time I spent overseas with Carl, when we were just married, and he was stationed in Germany. I didn't understand at the time—terribly ignorant when I was young."

Rueful laugh. "Aren't we all?"

A snort. "My granddaughter seems to know everything—certainly knows more about—" The throaty voice dropped to a subterranean level.

Robert tipped his head to peer between the wall of books. Yep. The librarian was nodding, even as she ran the wand over each book, then dropped it into a box.

Beatrice's face rose in his mind as a knot tightened in his stomach, the pain in her eyes puzzling him.

"You don't understand!"

What did he need to understand? He loved her, and she loved him, and they were married, after all. What more did she want? They had a couple of kids and didn't want more—at least not for a long while. Kelly and Roger were great, but even he could see how stressed Beatrice got with their schedules. He tried to help. But there was only so much he could do.

"It's not that!"

He had tried to hug her into a better mood, but she wasn't having it. Stiff as a board and just as unrelenting. Tears dripped down her face as she stared at the floor, slumped on the edge of the bed like some kind of broken toy.

Frustration filled him. Almost every night, it was the same routine. He approached, and she resisted. He cajoled until she either got mad or gave in.

"What's the deal? I thought Fridays were good for you. Look, I'm a patient guy, but even the best of men need a little encouragement."

She'd just stared. That baleful look spearing him with hopeless injury.

The librarian's voice startled him. She stood at his right, peering at the thrillers he had shoved aside. "Anything I can help you with?"

Got anything on how to talk your wife into a romantic mood? he didn't say. "Uh, just looking. Trying to figure out what I want. Thrillers just not cutting it for me."

Sympathetic eyes stared into him.

Good Lord, how much do librarians know?

"If you want a suggestion?" It was the other woman, the patron with the heavy stack.

He shrugged, appearing open but not needy. Or so he hoped.

"Try Palmer's series. Historical fiction starting in the middle-ages but with a psychological twist. Kind of thrilling, but he's got depth, if you know what I mean."

Robert glanced at the librarian for confirmation.

The white head nodded in agreement. "Oh, yes. Palmer is good. Real family drama without the typical social motifs. The gritty stuff of life but without antiquated solutions."

A groan rose inside Robert. "I got enough grit in my life. Thanks."

A conspiratorial grin passed between the two women.

Burning heat rose in Robert's cheeks, as if he just realized that he had forgotten to zipper his pants this morning. His left hand slowly inched onto his lap.

The librarian tried again. "Well, there's always Susan Price Marks Siva. She's got some fun escapism. Very global and internationally acclaimed." Her brows scrunched—trying to remember or trying to discern? "Thrilling but educational."

"You like biographies? There are some heart-stopping accounts on the shelf right behind myths and legends." The helpful patron jogged aside and pulled a heavy volume from the shelf. "Life and lies of—"

The door creaked open, and the three-some froze. Caught blatantly chattering in the library.

Tentative padding steps. Then a small voice. "Hello?"

What a sweet sound. An image of an apple tree in springtime rose in Robert's mind.

A blond head poked around the corner. A bright smile. The young woman stepped forward, a book lifted in her right hand. "I'm here to pay my debt to society."

Duty calling, the librarian returned to the counter, leading the way to reparation for overdue books.

Helpful patron chimed in. "I mark the due dates on my calendar. Got fined twice before I thought to do it. Funny how I have to make mistakes a few times before I learn how to solve them. O, happy fault, maybe?"

Robert didn't have a clue what the well-read woman was talking about. But as she turned and meandered to the fantasy section, he didn't follow up.

With a sigh, he replaced the thrillers in their proper section and wandered toward the counter.

The pretty lady stood with one arm propped on her hip, her body tilted, like a mother used to carrying a baby and can't get comfortable in a straight position.

"Dan's watching them. You know how it is. He loves the procreation process and playing with 'em when they're young, but the follow-up's a real chore."

The librarian met Robert's fixed stare as he stood one bookshelf away. Then she returned her gaze to the conversation at hand. "Growing up is hard. At every stage." She tapped the book. "You want to return this or renew it?"

A quiet sigh. "Well, I just got into it, but I never know if I'll get a chance to finish it. Between Dan and the kids, I get so tired, don't have any time to let my mind roam. My soul is not my own." She released a brittle, suck-it-up, chuckle. "But like you said—growing up is hard. Renew it, and I'll try to squeeze in a bit of time."

Stunned by the image of a captured, weary soul, Robert waited and then watched the young wife and mother saunter out the door. His gaze trailed after her as her blond head bobbed and then disappeared around the corner.

He marched forward and faced the librarian. "You have anything on 'Oh happy fault?'"

Breaking into a grin, the librarian pointed to the religion and philosophy section. "Probably. We've got something for everyone. Just have to figure out what you want."

A happy wife rang in Robert's ears. He lifted his hand. "You know, I better get going. Thanks. But I think the book I need to read—is at home."

He paced out the door and sauntered outside, a new story filling his mind.

Life's Storms

Originally published on The Writings of A. K. Frailey
3/26/2021

Kiara loved the sound of the wind rushing through the woodland. Earthy and rustic, it spoke of invisible worlds and steadfast powers beyond human control. Blades of spring grass poked up from last winter's mulch, and buds swelled in the promise of better things to come. She sighed. *If only…*

The sun had crested over an hour ago, and she must return to her apartment, then off to her shrill, insistent workplace, always maintaining a calm, professional demeanor.

A redbird alighted on a fence post, chirping an attractive, lilting tune. *Why can't I be a bird?*

"Kiara?"

Her sister's voice. Myra always knew where to look.

Kiara stepped from the shadows into the field. "Yes?"

"There you are!" Myra jogged forward. "Let's go to the lake. Mother left a cold supper in the kitchen, and the boys won't be back for another couple of hours."

A thrill ignited Kiara's imagination. "You think we could?" Doubt quickly cooled the spark to mere ash. "But I should prepare for—"

"Another workday?" Myra gripped her sister's arm and tugged. "You're always working, and when you die, your spirit will float about this beautiful planet, wondering why you ever lived."

Aching pressure surged against an inner wall, splashing over the ramparts. Tears filled Kiara's eyes.

~~~

The two women stood on the rocky shore, surrounded by cliffs held together by a phalanx of trees, ripples scurrying across the blue-green water.

A tall, lean man strolled toward them, waves splashing his toes.

Shock filled Kiara as she stared wide-eyed. "What's Jagan doing here?"

Myra kept her eyes glued to the horizon. "Does he have to have a reason?"

Images of the muddy water, floating debris, homes half-submerged in the flooded plain filled her mind. So many had lost loved ones in the disaster. The funerals never seemed to end. Then they did, and everyone returned to work and normal lives.

Normal? What does that mean? "I thought he moved up north, away from—"

Myra shot her a glance. "He did. But now he's back."

"He doesn't have family here. Not anymore."

Scuffing a bare toe against a smooth rock, Myra rubbed a fish-shaped pendant hanging around her neck. "Doesn't he?"

With a snort, Kiara tossed her head.

Jagan stopped and nodded. His eyes reflected grief mingled with endurance. "I was down the shore and saw you; hope I'm not interrupting."
~~~

Myra hugged her sister's arm. "Of course not. Mother has made enough supper for a spring festival; come and join us. The boys would love to see you. They've been working on a kite."

His gaze glancing off Kiara, Jagan waited.

Words tumbled from Kiara's lips before she knew what she was about. "Certainly. Come and be welcome. I have to return to work so someone should enjoy—" *What? Life?* She blushed in confusion.

Ignoring the unfinished thought, Jagan fell in step between the two women as they headed back to a small blue Honda. "You're still at the same place?"

Kiara nodded. "Same work. Same family. Same everything."

Myra's tiny head shake obliterated the lie. The petite woman pulled out her keys and slid into the driver's seat. "You two sit in back, and don't tell me how to drive."

~~~

After supper, Jagan met Kiara in the kitchen as she wiped the wooden table free of spots and crumbs. He tugged a towel off the rack and started drying the dishes. "Keeping busy helps, doesn't it?"

Her throat tightening, Kiara kept her gaze glued to the polished surface.

"I moved away. Thought I'd find peace if I didn't have to run into a memory every time I turned around."
~~~

The distant sound of rumbling thunder echoed off the hills. "But now you've returned. For good?"

He smiled and lifted the clean stack of plates onto the middle shelf. "For good? That's funny. I hardly know."

With a shrug, Kiara dismissed his honesty. "I like to keep busy. Productive." She squeezed the sponge and laid it neatly on the soap dish. "Not a problem."

Jagan leaned against the sink and nodded. "That's good. I hated it when I couldn't feel anything anymore. Just a vague unease, like something was supposed to be inside of me that wasn't."

The wind picked up, and branches swished against each other, groaning in stormy delight.

A shiver ran down Kiara's arms. "I should've headed back to my apartment this afternoon, but I got caught up in the spring sunshine. And Myra and Mom wanted...you know." She sighed. "I'll have to get up extra early tomorrow to make the drive if I want to get to work on time and do stuff."

With a playful twinkle, Jagan twitched the towel at Kiara. "Love doing stuff, do ya?"

Laughter bubbled inside Kiara. "You betcha! The more stuff, the better! I'm one of the best stuffers—" Suddenly, as if she had been stripped of every article of clothing like in a horrible nightmare, left without a single defense, choking tears killed all joy.

Jagan didn't ask. He simply took her in his arms and held her. Softly, without possession, advice, or comment.

Her tears stained his brown shirt, but she couldn't stop them. She hung on and let the tears do their work. After a deep calming breath, she pulled away. "I still have to go tomorrow."

He nodded. "And you'll manage another productive day."

"I will." She looked up and met his eyes. "And you?"

"I'm home now. Grief can find me whether I work or play."

Rain pounded the roof and beaded the window. A breeze sashayed into the kitchen.

"I wish I were a bird..."

Jagan took her hand, led her to the doorway, and flung open the door. Messy drops drizzled and splattered.

He pointed to the treetops where a nest swayed in the wind.

Queasiness unsettled Kiara's balance. "How do they stand it?"

He gripped her hand tighter. "It's home."

"Home?"

"The place where you face life's storms."

As the drops slowed, Kiara relaxed, peace enveloping her. *Home isn't a place. It's a presence.* For the first time in forever, her soul flew.

Don't Get Blown Away

Originally published on The Writings of A. K. Frailey
3/12/2021

Gray clouds, gusty winds, and flapping curtains—frantic, as if no one was listening—held Aisling on the threshold, waiting, but for what, she could not say.

Her husband, Diarmuid, hustled an overfilled wheelbarrow across the yard. His muscles strained with the effort, though he whistled a lively tune while he worked.

At the back of the greening-up yard, along the still-winter-dead hedgerow, her youngest son, Collin, swung on a frayed rope tied from a high branch. A dip in the land allowed him to free fall, enjoying the heady drop without any real danger.

Neither husband nor son seemed the least bit concerned about the pending storm. A neighbor had mentioned as they passed the post office that morning, "Lots of rain coming. Eager spring planters best hold off a bit, or every seed'll be washed away."

A sharp crack and snapping branches caught Aisling's attention. A damaged tree that had kept a stretched roothold into the bank of the ever-widening river had given way and was now lodged in the crook of a straight but world-weary tree.

Having dumped his load of compost, Diarmuid looked over, a rake motionless in his hand. "Ya see that?"

Aisling nodded.

Collin pelted across the yard, a spring kite off its tether, his shirttail flapping behind him. He skidded to a stop at the crumbling bank. "Hey, da! See what it's done!"

Aisling met her husband at the crooked river bend where the tree fell and got caught.

"It's them strangling vines that done it. They're taking over the back lot, sucking up the water and soil, so even the young starve where they stand."

A swift kick to the gut could not have stunned Aisling more. Dread chased logic right out of her mind. "Niamh got the job."

Darkness deepened the glint in Diarmuid's eyes. "I hope she knows what she's about. There's no telling what life'll be like that far from home. Can't harvest a garden in a city apartment."

Motherly defenses rising, Aisling crossed her arms, a barricade against fears that can't possibly understand. "It's her life. She has to find her own way."

"The land holds true when people fail."

A gust of wind toppled a chair on the porch, sending Collin sprinting across the yard. "I'll get it. Just hope the house don't blow away!"

With a sharp turn, Diarmuid paced back to the half-tilled garden.

Under her breath, Aisling prayed. "I hope so too."

~~~

Late that night, as the house stood quiet and the curtains hung limp and lifeless, Aisling wiped the counter and wrung the dishrag dry. She lay it on the edge of the clean sink, took a last glance
~~~

around the orderly kitchen, and turned off the light. She headed for bed.

Moonlight shone through Collin's window, and the toe of his boot glinted from under a chair.

She padded down the hallway, the sound of the shower grew louder in her ears. In the master bedroom, she peeled off her shoes and socks and then readied her bedclothes. Her computer screen had gone to sleep, but she knew there were emails and financial business to attend to early the next morning. A stack of biographies, novels, and historical epics lay beside the bed. Lots to read, to imagine, to consider, but her exhausted brain couldn't fathom anything more than her bedtime ritual.

The shower spray stopped with a sudden halt, the floorboards groaned, and she could imagine Diarmuid drying off in his own methodical way.

Everything was peaceful now, and Aisling wondered at her dread-filled fears during the storm. She searched her mind for the emotional landmines that had sent her down such a treacherous rabbit hole. Niamh's new job? She shook her head and pulled down the covers on the bed. There was no reason to fear that a grown woman living a mere hundred miles away would come to a bad end just because she worked in the city.

The bathroom door opened, and Diarmuid, dressed in his sweat pants and little else, strolled in, toweling off his hair. "We'll have to take two cars. She'll need one till she gets settled in. And there's a zoo near the place Collin might like. We can make a weekend of it. Once she finds out what life is like there, she might appreciate home a bit more."

Aisling nodded. There was no arguing her husband's brand of logic.

She plodded to the bathroom, stripped, got into the shower, and turned it on piping hot. Luxuriating in the steaming spray, Collin's words ran in her mind: *hope the house don't get blown away.*

Suddenly her fear made perfect sense. She wasn't afraid of losing her daughter but losing the home her daughter could return to.

Her home.

Her life.

What makes my life? My home?

"Hey, honey, where'd you put my reading glasses?"

Aisling smiled at a memory. "You left them by the printer this morning when you got the paper stuck, remember?"

"Oh. Yeah. That."

She heard his chuckle and knew he had remembered too. She slipped on her nightclothes, brushed her teeth, and shuffled into the bedroom.

Diarmuid sat propped against a pile of pillows, a biography in his hand. He looked over his glasses and peered at her. "You doing okay?"

A gust of wind hit the house and startled the curtains.

But the house still stood.

A deep abiding peace settled Aisling's soul. "Yeah. Life's good. I like your idea about taking two cars and visiting the zoo. I'm going to take a tomato plant in a crate so Niamh can have a little bit of home in her apartment."

"Huh. Nice thought, but it won't be the same."

"No. But we all have to start somewhere. Then we start building and try not to get blown away."

Those Pesky Black Holes

Originally published on The Writings of A. K. Frailey
2/26/2021

"Sucked into Black Holes During Sleep, They Share Their Darkest Secrets."

Bruno read the headline twice, promptly running his cart into the store shelf. Stunned, he jerked his gaze off his phone.

"Hey, not supposed to read while driving." A woman, fifties, blunt-cut, short hair, laughed with shining eyes.

Shocked, Bruno stashed his phone in his pocket and shoved his cart alongside the shelf, a guilty child trying to hide the evidence. He forced a grin. No words were forthcoming.

She sidled up, her smile dimming by degrees. "Sorry. I tried to warn you. But you were so intent—"

He scratched his head. He didn't want to have a conversation. A lie formed before his conscience could object. "I had to check a text—"

She lifted a hand. "Not my business. I was being stupid." Her gaze took in the contents of his cart.

Dang it. An extra-large bag of his dad's Depends and a bright blue denture cleaner box bared the naked side of human misery. In revenge, he snuck a look at her cart. Red hair dye and blue nail polish. He glanced at her. Gray hair, fingers unadorned. He frowned.

She grimaced. "My mom's dealing with that crap too. She was at Wayside, but with everything, I brought her home and got home healthcare. It's better, but not really good, if you know what I mean."

Relief, like a spring breeze, washed over Bruno. "Dad's still on his own, sort of. Lives in the apartment above me. Neither of us can give up our independence. But..."

She snatched up the box of dye. "She gets bored and depressed. So, every couple of months, I do a new treatment. This month—" Her lips flapped as she blew a puff of air. "Rad red! I'd like to take her out to eat or something—"

Bruno shrugged in compassionate understanding. "Hell trying to keep 'em on their feet."

She snorted but a smile crept back into her eyes. "It was easier with a toddler. I could toss them into a cart and strap 'em in."

"My twins gave me weekly heart attacks, but they grew out of their hijinks." Bruno tried not to let the next thought tear his heart out.

With a commander's wave, she redirected her cart. "Well, best of luck then, and keep an eye out for where you're heading."

"Ha. I'll be more careful." *I'm not going anywhere.*

~~~

Bruno flipped three grilled cheese sandwiches and then stirred a pot of creamy tomato soup. "Lunch is ready, Dad."

His dad hobbled in. Using his cane with deft power, he nudged a kitchen chair aside and plunked down at the table with a long sigh.
~~~

"Smells good. He stretched his neck, peering at the pot. "You add something extra?"

"Lots of garlic salt." He slid one sandwich onto a plate and placed it on the table. Then he poured the soup into a wide bowl and set it alongside. He fixed his own meal, grabbed a couple of spoons, and dropped them into place. He plopped down on a chair across from his dad, folded his hands, and bowed his head.

Hurried sign of the cross, a quick prayer, and they started in.

Slurps and clanks of metal on glass accompanied their chewing and swallowing.

The old man glanced up, wiped his chin, and huffed. "Anything new in the big world?"

Bruno shrugged as he swallowed his last bite. "I ran into a shelf and some strange woman laughed at me."

His eyes widening in horror, the old man spluttered, "The wretched—"

Bruno grinned. "I wasn't looking where I was going, and she was nice enough." He pulled out his phone. "I wanted to check something, and I got stopped by a headline—something about people falling into a black hole. Caught my attention at a weak moment. Smack. Hit the toothpaste shelf full speed."

Grinning, the old man rested his spoon on his empty bowl and tucked the used napkin underneath. "Good thing you didn't hit a middle aisle. You could've set off a cascade of cat food." He frowned. "What were you checking?"

A blush burned Bruno's face. "There was such a variety of adult diapers. I had no idea."

Dropping his gaze, a flush darkened his dad's cheeks. "Aw, hell. I wish—"

"Don't, dad. It's not so bad. Everyone has stuff to deal with. That woman's mom is depressed and needs a new perm every month." He leaned in and dropped his voice to a conspiratorial whisper. "And likes to have her nails done. I'll take a bag of Depends over that any day."

The old man's hand shook as he reached across the table and pressed his son's fingers.

~~~

Though dark clouds scuttled in from the north and the temperature was dropping, there was still enough time to get in one more lap around the park. Bruno shook the last vestiges of tension from his shoulders and focused on a pair of squirrels chasing each other around a tree.

He promptly bumped shoulders with a woman jogging by on his left.

Huffing, she scowled and stopped. "Hey! Look where—"

She looked strangely familiar. Embarrassment and dripping sweat sent an uncomfortable chill down Bruno's back. "Sorry. I was—"

"Oh, you again." A smile quirked her lips. "But you're not texting and driving, at least. Thank God for that."

A park bench behind the central swing set beckoned.

"I'm ready for a break. You?"
~~~

She nodded. “Sure. Mom’s napping, so I sneak out on the weekends to get in a little R & R.”

Trudging across the dead winter grass, he puffed a laugh. “You call running rest and relaxation?”

She plodded alongside. “Don’t you?”

He waited while she brushed broken twigs aside and plopped down.

They breathed freely for a few moments, gazing at the quiet park.

A trio of squirrels scampered past.

Bruno wagged his finger. “It was their fault, really. I got caught up in their drama.”

Laughter filled the park. A happy sound. She settled into a giggle. “Yeah, it’s always something, isn’t it?”

He turned. “How’s your mom doing?”

She blinked and swallowed. “Okay. Not really thrilled with the red. She wants to go back to being a blond, but with her wispy threads, it wouldn’t be pretty. Need something to distract the eye, if you know what I mean.” Changing course, she clapped one mittened hand over the other and focused on him. “And your dad. How’s he?”

“Scarfs down my grilled cheese and tomato soup like it’s going out of style.”

A fresh laugh, softer, but honest and appreciative.

Two plump robins hopped nearby.

He nudged her and signaled with his eyes.

She smiled. “Wish I brought something. Breadcrumbs...”

He nodded.

She cleared her throat. “You ever bring your dad out to eat? Like to your kids’ place or—”

He tipped his head. “I would, but they live in California. An airport would be a nightmare.” He cut his glance aside. “Yours?”

“Naw. They’re not very patient with her. Nice enough when I do everything, but they’re mostly eat-outers.”

Like a bobblehead, he just nodded a bit.

The clouds parted, and a ray of sunshine illuminated the park, bathing the playground in golden light.

She spoke to the sky. “I have a ramp up to the kitchen door. A neighbor helped with it. Got treads and everything.”

“Me too.”

Two of the squirrels perched on a branch, sitting amiably. The third bounded toward the swings.

“Your mom likes grilled cheese?”

Though her head stayed down, a smile lit her face brighter than sunshine. “She loves it.” She looked over, shifting in her seat, getting a firmer position. “I make a fantastic beef stew. Really easy to chew but nutritious as all get out.”

“Really?” He pulled out his phone. “You know, I read that black holes have been catching people while they sleep. Thought maybe you’d like to help me keep watch out for ‘em.” He cleared his throat, scrounging up his courage. “Maybe we could have dinner together sometime—your mom, my dad—us.”

A glimmer entered her eyes as her smile widened. “Oh, yeah. Got to keep our eye out for those pesky black holes. They swallow people alive, I hear, unless we help each other out."

He stood and pointed across the park. "My place is just there. Dad's got his own ideas about things—but he's feisty enough to keep black holes at bay. Care to meet him?"

She stood and squared her shoulders. "Only if you're willing to meet my mom. God knows what color her hair will be."

He laughed as he nudged her forward. "Long as she hasn't been swallowed whole—she'll be all right with me."

Between Worlds

Originally published on The Writings of A. K. Frailey
2/12/2021

Shailyn jerked upright in bed, jolted from the other world back into her own. The usual, odd discomfort dogged her as she peeled back the heavy bed covers, then trod to the bathroom for her daily ablutions.

I belong there haunted her thoughts as she tugged on her jeans and a heavy sweater, though she knew, realistically, she couldn't live there. As a between-worlder, she was powerless to pick a permanent lodging.

Shivering in the cold morning air, she plodded to the kitchen and gratefully poured herself a cup of steaming coffee. Her daughter, Win, always got up first and made sure that the pot was full and piping hot before she left for work. *Bless that girl.*

She retreated to the comfort of the living room, Shailyn added a log to the burning embers in the woodstove and sat on the sturdy rocker before the big bay windows. February rain slanted across the glass as pine boughs swayed against the gray sky.

Misty, her daughter's tiny pup, scampered into the room and leapt into her lap, squirming with all the energy of young life.

In a valiant effort to keep her coffee from spilling, Shailyn nudged the quadruped to a comfortable spot on her lap, took a sip of the dark brew, and then sat back and closed her eyes. Dream images of herself traipsing along the muddy bank of a beautiful lake, a distant, untidy cottage, and a huge water bird charging with flapping wings over a line dug in the earth while intoning, "*Stay where you belong!*" sent confused sensations rippling over her body.

Pounding steps echoed down the staircase. Her eldest, Morgan, tromped to the kitchen, splashed coffee into his oversized mug, and then meandered to her side. His hair disheveled and dressed in dark jeans, a pullover sweater, and boots, he peered over his cup as he took his first hurried gulp.

Shailyn waited. She knew what was coming. Just like she knew what her answer would be. Though she'd have to gather strength from somewhere else to make her words believable.

"You'll be there to pick her up, right?"

"Absolutely. Once I get my old bones ready to face the day."

"May's going to need all the help she can get, but I have to handle the newest crises breaking out at work."

"You take care of your business, and I'll do mine."

A snort turned Shailyn's gaze from the tears streaming down the window pane.

"Technically, she's not your responsibility. She's *my* stepdaughter." He shook his head. "If only—"

"Stop!" She couldn't handle if-onlys today. There was no changing the past. No bringing the dead back to life. She glanced at her son's weary, wounded soul peeking through his gray-green eyes. "She's all our responsibility—everyone who has a heart to love, should."

"It's a lot to ask—by all rights, you'd be in retirement now, enjoying your last days, not taking care of a disabled kid."

The wind picked up as rage surged through Shailyn. "She's not a disabled kid! She's a wounded child. Just like you're a wounded man, though your wounds are on the inside."

Chastened, Morgan swallowed the last drops and eyed his mom. "Most are." He trod to the kitchen, placed the cup on the counter, and called out as he yanked open the door. "She'll be ready at ten. The nurse will have all her stuff packed, and they'll fold and load the wheelchair for you, so don't mess with it. May can walk into the house with help. Just get her settled downstairs. I'll do the rest when I get home."

The picture of May's imploring, chocolate-brown eyes following her as she puttered around the house sent shivers down her arms. She frowned and bit her lip.

A glittery box stuffed into the bookshelf caught her eye. Jessica from church thought that she'd enjoy an "epic puzzle" in her old age and had sent her one with a thousand pieces. She nudged the pup's warm body from her lap and rose to her feet. She waved to her son through the window.

~~~

The box-cover picture, a fairy child plucking a blue flower under the umbrella of a wide, red-spotted mushroom, while raindrops splattered against the sheltering roof and vibrant grass
~~~

stems bent in gentle perfection, soothed Shailyn's soul.

May pressed a border piece into place, her eyes shining at the mighty accomplishment. "I got this side done."

"You're quick. I'm only halfway through my edge."

"They gave me lots of puzzles to do at the hospital." May's gaze traveled to the couch loaded with stuffed animals and three colorful blankets. "Giving me stuff makes them feel better, I think."

Shailyn held a corner piece and considered her options. "There's nothing wrong with trying to help. Or attempting to make you feel better."

"They couldn't keep mom alive or fix my back." She shrugged. "Not in this world."

Shailyn pressed her piece into place and sat back. She rubbed her cold hands. "I'm going to stoke the fire and check the stew. You want anything while I'm up?"

"You have any chocolate milk?"

"I've got milk and cocoa packets. If I get wild and mix them—well, we'll see what happens."

A grin peeked through May's eyes.

~~~

Darkness had laid the landscape still and silent by the time Morgan slipped in the back door. He shoved the wheelchair against the wall and unfolded it, ready for action.

Shailyn met him in the kitchen. "There's stew left. Though you're lucky. May managed to work her way through two bowlfuls, much to my amazement."
~~~

Staring through haggard eyes, Morgan pulled off his coat and tossed it on a chair. "She always amazes me. Like her mom. Resilient beyond belief."

Until she wasn't.

Shailyn shook her head. "Sit down and take a rest. I'll get it for you." She glanced at the ceiling, giving due notice to the room above. "She went to bed at eight-thirty. Not a peep since." Shailyn pulled a plastic container from the refrigerator and poured the chunky liquid into a glass bowl. She placed it in the microwave and hit two.

Morgan leaned on the worn wooden table, resting his head on his hand. "She do okay? And you—it wasn't too much?"

"Define too much." Shailyn shrugged. "She put half a puzzle together at the speed of lightning, slurped down a large chocolate milk, put away two bowls of stew, and agreed to my syllabus for home school for the rest of the semester."

"Ma, you sure you want—"

The microwave beeped repeatedly, warning that it could keep stew hot only so long.

Morgan stood and waved his mom off. "Sit; relax. I'll get it." He pulled the hot stew from the microwave, rummaged in the cupboard for bread, and plunked down on his chair, ready to dig into his assembled meal. He took a large scoop, savored it, and then stared at his mom, his eyebrows finishing his question.

Shailyn peeled a banana and sat opposite. "I'm hardly the best teacher in the world, but I can help her through her online classes. We don't know what next year will look like, but for now, this is where she should be. You and Win manage this big, old rambling house; I keep it stocked with healthy dinners and fun snacks. We're family. What else should I be doing—putting bigger puzzles together?"

"You could be traveling, seeing the world, visiting friends..."

"I could be laying in the cemetery, cold and stiff. Lots of could be's. All fantasy. What is—makes the world go around. I'm right where I belong."

His shoulders relaxing as the weight of a grievous month lifted just a bit, Morgan offered a lopsided grin.

~~~

After dressing in comfortable, warm sweats in the quiet of her room, Shailyn stretched out on her bed, turned off the light, pulled her blanket over her shoulders, and slipped into dreams that would take her away but could never keep her.
~~~

Richly Blessed

Originally published on The Writings of A. K. Frailey
1/29/21

"He will be missed."

Jacob read the quote twice before he put the fragile newspaper aside. Cleaning had never been his favorite job, but after his grandma passed two months before, he knew that he couldn't sell her old farmhouse until it was completely cleaned out, and that meant sorting through all the junk from her past. A long past full of cards, letters, mementos, pictures, and even Great-Granddad's old house key. The woman saved everything.

He sighed, shifted his crouched position in the dim, dusty attic, and glanced at the carefully cut-out article again. Who was this man that she bothered to save his obituary? And was he really missed? He had died so long ago, those who cared were long gone. *Doesn't matter now.*

"Jacob?"

Rosie's voice, melodic and enticing, still sent chills up his arms. He could hardly believe she had married him and that they were expecting their first child in the spring. After sweeping the last stacks of papers off the shelf, Jacob bundled them into the over-filled plastic container and grunted as he hefted it to the top of the steps. "This is the last of it. I'm coming down now."

With her rounded belly giving shape to her bright maternity top, Rosie peered up from the bottom step. "Don't carry too much. You might fall."

With a half-laugh, Jacob defied the silly notion and started down the narrow steps, slipped on the fifth, and landed with decided "Ugh!" and a sharp pain in his back.

As if to add insult to injury, the box tipped and spilled its guts all over the floor.

Suddenly commander and chief of healthcare, Rosie dove into action, her hands fluttering. "Stop! Stay where you are. Let me see if your—"

Ignoring her attention, Jacob tried to stand, then muffled a series of profanities as he fell again.

By late afternoon, Jacob had been x-rayed, found he had slipped a disk, and was sentenced to bed for the duration with enough pain killer and vegetable soup to keep him alive though not uncomplaining.

~~~

After arriving at their single-story ranch home, Rosie made the necessary phone calls, informing work, family, and friends that her "strong-man" was doing fine, though he wouldn't be getting around for a few days.

Jacob could hear her voice from the bedroom as she prepared dinner, soothing away worries, insisting that she didn't need any help, and glorying in the fact that she had tried to warn him, "But you know how he is..."

He considered popping another pill to dull the humiliation.

Cute as always but with a hint of smugness, Rosie toted in a tray just as the winter sun set. A roast beef sandwich with barbecue chips,
~~~

coleslaw, and a glass of milk gladdened his eyes, bringing his salivary glands back to life, though he looked twice at the glass of milk. A faded newspaper article lay complacently under the fork.

"You need extra calcium. The doctor specifically mentioned that you should drink milk and get more exercise."

Jacob's brain spun, trying to think of a non-profanity-laden retort.

"Oh, and Mrs. Miller put the box in the car and carried it into the living room so we could go through it." She tapped the paper. "I found this article on a great-great-uncle of yours. Sounds like he was quite a guy."

His brain had frozen at the image of Mrs. Miller carrying the box to the car. "The woman is seventy-six years old! How could she carry—"

"Very carefully. She wouldn't let me touch it because of the baby. And she knows how much we want to get the house cleaned out. Her son said he'd bring his boys over, you know the twins, Jim and Jerry, to do the last of the patching and painting. Then it'll be fit for the realtor to put on the market."

Picturing the middle-aged brothers, grizzled farmers who lived down the lane, Jacob stifled a groan. *When did my life slip out of control?* "Really, I think we should hire someone to—"

Rosie perched on the edge of the bed and shook her head, eternally patient wise-woman. "Don't be ridiculous. There isn't a carpenter to be had—no professional wants to go into these old farmhouses unless you want a complete refurbish job. Which we can't afford. Jim and Jerry have done tons of work on their own place; they can handle this. We'll pay them, and the house will be fine." She nudged the milk closer, glanced pointedly at the article, and climbed to her feet. "Eat and rest. I'm going to see how many hearts and likes we got on Facebook."

Oh, heck... Jacob shoved the Facebook humiliation out of his mind and chomped down his meal. He ignored the article. But as he couldn't eat it, there wasn't a television or a computer within reach, and he had left his phone in the car, his fingers inched toward the yellowed newspaper.

He read it three times. His eyes filled with tears on the second round and flowed after the third. How could he have had such a relative and never heard? But then he remembered. Grandma had spoken of her Uncle Thomas, a priest who had served his flock in love and devotion, who had died unexpectedly. But he had never paid it much mind. Some old relative who had passed away long before his time.

Rosie hummed as she switched off the last of the lights, waddling closer, her happy disposition radiating through the house.

Suddenly, Jacob envisioned the web of interconnected lives. The great uncle who had powerfully influenced his mother, who had formed him. The long descent of relatives who arrived and left the human stage in numberless succession, changing the landscape for each generation.

Rosie stopped in the doorway; her eyes widened in alarm as she stared at him. "What's wrong, honey?" She hustled close, arms ready to snuggle and comfort.

Jacob breathed her unique scent, soaked in her gentle touch, and knew, beyond all shadow of a doubt, he had been richly blessed.

Together Again

Originally published on The Writings of A. K. Frailey
1/15/2021

Charles would never be able to look his sister in the eyes again. He stared at the slumped form in the cage and whistled low. *It can't be.* But it was. Dead.

Once he had cleared out a nest of mice from the garage, so the irony of failing as a hamster caretaker struck everything but the funny bone.

Three years ago, Robin had been diagnosed with cancer, one that might prove fatal or might go into remission forever. A chancy thing that Charles could not understand even after researching it online till his eyes ached.

This last hospital stay meant that someone had to take care of Henny.

He had said he would.

And he had meant it.

But life got in the way, and he forgot.

Now Henny lay like a petrified rock before an empty feed bowl. Dried crust rings adorned the empty water dish.

Mom's voice raced up the stairs. "Charles?"

He had to answer. He was in Robin's room. Mom wouldn't ask about Henny. *Never cross her mind.* "Yeah?"

"Dad and I are going now. The hospital said that one of us could pop in for a visit if we get there in the hour."

No explanation needed. He knew all the restrictions and why he was not on the short list of visitors. "Fine."

“Bye, honey. Keep an eye on the chicken in the crockpot.”

The front door shut with all the force of a late winter wind behind it.

Charles sighed. He opened the cage and did the needful. Despite the frozen ground, he’d give his sister’s pet a decent burial. It was the least he could do.

~~~

Online classes set Charles’ nerves on edge. There were so many more interesting things he could be doing with his time. He googled hamsters and discovered that there were a few within his price range. No one would know...except Robin, of course. She had a mama-bear’s sensitivity. One whisker out of place, and her eyebrows would rise sky high.

He sighed and drummed his fingers on his desk. How on earth could he replace hamster-love? Clearly, with her frequent hospital visits, another pet wasn’t a good option. A game? How about a craft they could do together? She liked nature walks—he could take her to the park every week. Or a boyfriend? He could set her up with—Charles shook his head. She was only twelve, for heaven’s sake. *What am I thinking?*

His phone buzzed, and his stomach tightened. Either his teacher or his mom. Nether a welcome distraction. He checked his text messages.
~~~

Hey, Sweetie! Great news. They're letting us take her home today. Just got a few things to finish up, and we'll all be together again.

Surprise!!!!!

Get the chicken ready, and Dad will pick up some dessert on the way to celebrate.

Hearts and smiles,

~Mom

If a national emergency had been declared, and he was being sent to the front lines, Charles' heart could not have pounded any harder.

~~~

From the sound of boots stomping into the living room, hearty laughter, and voices chattering way too loud, Charles knew something was off. He had cleaned up the remains of Henny's house; her empty cage stood in the corner of his closet, out of sight. He hoped out of mind.

He had changed his dirty shirt and finished his biology assignment—one focused on rodents—only adding to life's cruel fate.

He sucked in a deep breath and marched down stairs.

Mom was bustling in every direction, humming some ridiculous tune in the kitchen, and Dad was helping Robin get settled on the couch. Lots of pillows and extra blankets.

Oh, God.

Twelve? She looked eighty. Her sunken eyes peered at him as a smile quivered on her lips.
~~~

Brave but doomed. He knew it. She knew it. And now she knew that he knew it.

Henny's slumped form flashed before his eyes, and a lump rose to his throat. He forced it down, strode to the couch, and plunked down beside her. In his fifteen-years on earth, it was the bravest thing he had ever done.

He nudged her shoulder.

She nudged him back. Her smile widened and real this time.

"So, you've come back to plague me with song requests, I suppose? Twenty new tunes you want uploaded?"

"Only seven—but I found a game we can play. You just have to set it up."

Huge, long-suffering sigh. He nudged her again.

Mom called from the kitchen, "Dinner's ready!" with all the practice of a spring lark. All hell could be breaking loose, but as long as she had dinner ready, cheerfulness reigned supreme.

Dad sprang into action, his arm ready, his hovering presence all that Robin needed to get to the kitchen table.

Eating wasn't difficult. It was impossible. But Charles managed it anyway.

A Netflix movie—a Jane Austin romance that made Charles and his dad exchange eye-rolls every other scene—and evening prayers completed the night.

Sweating bullets every time Robin offered an inquisitive glance in his direction, Charles prayed that she'd forget about Henny until tomorrow.

No such luck.

Ascending the steps, she clutched her dad's hand and hit Charles square between the eyes. "How's Henny been? I feel bad, leaving her so long. But I'm sure you've taken good care. She's so silly."

What does silly have to do with it? She wasn't a silly hamster. She was a rodent. Nothing to shed tears over. His vision blurred. "Can you wait till tomorrow? I'm really tired tonight."

She nodded. "Me too." She slipped off to bed.

Laying in the dark, facing the monsters chasing him down the corridors of his imagination, Charles knew his days were numbered. He couldn't live through this. He didn't want to.

~~~

After a night of dreams skewered by nonsense nightmares, Charles swallowed each bite of cereal in the same way that a camel manages with cactus leaves. Ignore the prickles and force it on down.

Dad, his protective armor on, patted Charles' back as he strode into the kitchen. "You doing okay?"

There was no good answer, so Charles simply shrugged.

The phone buzzed. A loud conversation upstairs, Mom's laughter, and then Mom skittering downstairs with the phone held out. "Jason has everything set, but he wants us there to make sure it's what we want. Then he'll bring it over right after he gets it loaded."
~~~

Apparently, the message made sense to Dad. He nodded, grabbed his coat, and snatched his keys.

Mom leaned in to Charles. "She's still sleeping. We won't be gone long. If she wakes up, get her something to eat so she doesn't try to take the stairs, okay? We're getting the bed the doctor recommended, so she'll be more comfortable."

After an affirming nod, they were out the door.

Silence pervaded the house for the next fifteen minutes. Then the shuffling steps of a very old or very sick person padded overhead.

Charles trotted upstairs and rushed to his sister's room. But she wasn't there. He glanced at the bathroom. Empty. His heart thudded as he approached his room. There she stood, the closet door open, Henny's cage pulled out, empty and forlorn.

"I'm sorry. It was all my fault—"

Surprisingly strong, Robin's voice warbled across the room to the doorway. "She was three years old—that's ancient for a hamster."

But you're only twelve. Tears stung Charles' eyes.

She turned and faced him. "I was thinking...maybe you could walk outside and take pictures, text 'em, then call me, and describe stuff. Then—well—I won't miss spring completely."

Charles nodded.

~~~

All through February and deep into March, he sent pictures of Snowdrops, Crocus, maple buds,
~~~

early, eager bees, and the first robin to come bob-bobbing-along. She responded with hearts, googly-eyed smiling faces, and other ridiculous emojis that made him laugh out loud.

~~~

After the last thaw in mid-April when the temperatures finally rose again, he tread carefully across the slushy grass, box under his arm and a spade in hand. He stopped before the fresh mound. It might take years for grass to grow over the site. He clasped the stained container and, with the aid of his spade, made a small hole at the foot of the grave. He placed the box front and center, then covered it with all the care of an operating doctor finishing a procedure. He patted the earth and leaned on the spade handle.

"Together again, best I can arrange it. Dumb mistake to forget Henny...but sometimes, it's hard to see stuff."

A red-breasted robin hopped close and cocked its head.

Charles knelt on the muddy ground and lifted his hand. They stared at each other for a long moment.

Then it fluttered its wings and flew away.
~~~

New Generation

Originally published on The Writings of A. K. Frailey 1/1/2021

Elmer knew better than to believe in ghosts. But when he awoke with sweat beading on his forehead and the sensation that he had just returned from a long journey through wild-lands with only his body and wits intact, he knew that something otherworldly was at work.

His wife stirred at his side. She slapped the blankets, her face half-smashed against the pillow, her eyes squeezed shut. “Don’t get up…too early.”

Too early or too late? He pressed his chest, trying to steady his galloping heart. “Hon-honey?”

One eye opened. Not a flicker of interest.

“Do you remember going to a desert town with broken-down buildings and getting kidnapped?”

Lana sat up, groggily rubbing her fingers through her short tufts of hair.

Elmer swallowed the lump in his throat. *What happened to her luscious brown locks?*

She steered her gaze over her husband, taking the long tour. Dubious. Pity?

His hands shaking, Elmer threw off the wrinkled sheets and stalked to the bathroom. He swiped on the cold water, splashed his face, straightened, and snatched a towel. He wiped the drips running down his baggy t-shirt. *Have I lost weight?* He sucked in a shuddering breath. “What day is it?”

Lana padded across the bedroom. “Sunday, goof. New Year’s Day, remember?”

An electric bolt sizzled through his body. "N-new year?"

With a snarky laugh, Lana strolled into the bathroom wearing a calf-length night dress that should look sexy as hell but didn't.

Elmer stared. *Why?*

She leaned her head on his shoulder, a buddy-nudge, nothing wifely about it. "You remember the year, right?"

Terror gripped Elmer, nearly closing his throat. "Twenty-twenty—"

"Ha-ha! Got ja!" She smacked him, grinning like a lottery winner. "You had a whole year to get used to the thirties, and now you've slipped-up. Used to make fun of me!"

His gaze shifted from his wife to the mirror. *Where did these gray streaks come from?* His eyes—haggard and...vacant? *Lord, have mercy.*

Frowning, Lana shoved off and crossed her arms, the tilt of her body accenting the sharpness of her bony frame. "Twenty-thirty-one! We toasted and the VR bots cheered. Remember?"

Elmer slapped his face. "Ten years?" He retreated to the bedroom, marched to the window, and lifted the curtain. A barren square of dead grass met his eyes. Only a rotting stump stood in testimony of past life. "What the—" He turned and glared at Lana. "Where's our backyard?"

"Backyard?" She tiptoed forward and pressed her cold hand against his forehead. "You feeling all right?" She leaned in and stared deep into his eyes. "Time for your new-gen?"

A chill ran down his spine as he stared at the strange woman.

An elegant roll of the eyes. She flounced to the bedside, yanked open a drawer, and gripped a tube. She shook it, grinning. “You skipped your last dose—see what happens? Bad dreams, memory troubles... You need a pop and time inside.” Swinging the tube, she strode out of the bedroom.

His stomach dropped. Dragging it along behind, Elmer followed like a wary dog.

He faced what should have been his living room—a modern setup with overstuffed chairs, a broad couch, a large screen television centered on the back wall, matching end tables with iron lamps—opening to a large island-dominated kitchenet.

He froze.

Two worn chairs faced a bank of curved screens.

His gaze scraped the bare walls and gray floor. Cold. Dingy. Crumps, dust, stains, clutter. Broken family portraits lay scattered. One oil painting, ripped on the left side, stood propped on the floor, a forgotten project.

Elmer licked his lips. “Wh-where’s the Christmas tree?”

A snort and hollow laughter. “Christmas tree! What the hell is wrong with you?” She lumbered to the kitchen and dragged a chipped cup from the sink. She slapped the faucet, let water fill the container, plopped in a white pill, and watched it sizzle. She held out her offering. “Drink up!”

His whole body trembling, Elmer backed up, his hands raised. “What’s going on?”

Confusion raced irritation over Lana's face. "I've heard of memory lapses, but this is a bit much. What's the last thing you remember?"

Elmer edged his way to the nearest chair and plopped down, his body conforming to the seat, oddly comforting. "Christmas. We stopped at church for our ten-minute visit, came home, did our family video, then opened gifts. Jason gave us that new Virtual Reality Game..."

Lana sneered. "Ancient history, Elm. Christmas...church—mythology. Video chats for work, yeah, but who cares about family—it's only DNA." She wrinkled her nose and held out the cup.

He accepted it and sniffed. Nothing.

She tapped her wrist, bringing the screens to life. Rotating images flashed—a rainforest, a medieval castle, and a desert with broken-down buildings. "Time to get back to the real world."

~~~

Sucking in a heaving breath, Elmer shot up in bed, his heart racing. He glanced wildly around.

Lana, her long brown hair running riot over the blankets, lay on her side, her face in peaceful repose.

He heaved a long sigh and softly inched out of bed. Padding to the bathroom, he stared in the mirror. No gray streaks. A little bloodshot and brooding, but definitely his eyes. *Thank God.*

"Honey?"

Elmer froze.
~~~

“I’m so tired. Get me that New-gen Marge gave me last night, okay?”

Blinking, Elmer trotted to the living room and snatched the curtain away from the bank of windows. A soft blanket of snow covered their miniature backyard, the maple tree still standing in the center. Furniture, Christmas tree, paintings on the wall. Familiar. Home. He released a long breath.

“Honey?” Her voice had risen to a whine.

Like a wolf approaching a strange den, he sidled toward the kitchenet. The flash of a curved screen glinted from under the tree as he went by.

A red box with huge letters “A New Generation” screamed on the central island.

His fingers trembling, Elmer opened the box.

~~~

Elmer closed the door, padded to his bedroom, and flopped onto the bed.

Sitting propped against a bank of colorful pillows with a book in her hands, Lana peered at him through narrowed eyes. “I still don’t get why you had to have the whole family over.”

Elmer shrugged.

“And what happened to the new VR set Jason gave us?”

Elmer kicked off his shoes and slid back onto the pillows. He wrapped his arm around his wife’s shoulders. “We don’t need it.”

She shook her head. “Like Marge’s gift?” She laid the book on her lap. “You know, you’ve been a different guy since New Year’s Day.”
~~~

Elmer exhaled and pulled his wife close, his passion real and desire rising. “I hope so, sweetie. I hope so.”

For Me?

Originally published on The Writings of A. K. Frailey12/18/2020

An old woman and her grilled tuna sandwich saved my life. Not that I was starving. I wasn't. In fact, I hadn't had an appetite in three days. Moreover, I had no wish to live. She didn't know that. But, still, she wouldn't let me die.

Growing up back home, Mom reeked of respectability and intelligence. She could entertain a crowd, outpace a runaway train, and beat the devil himself to the punch line. And she could outdrink all the other moms at our daycare center. Her liver didn't appear to mind. Her brain cells did. But they didn't let on until much later.

The winter I turned twenty, my world froze hard and deep. Not that December was ever particularly warm in Chicago. But that year, the trip home to Milwaukee on the Greyhound bus left me shivering even after I got inside Mom's house. The holidays were tough. Lots of memories. Not the jolly kind. But I faced the season with all the joy I could muster. After all, Mom loved Christmas. It was the day after Christmas that got her down.

When I bustled through the door, a blue-green Christmas tree about six inches high with holes for lollipops stood on the phone stand. A rainbow of candies stuck out on each side, aching to send a diabetic into insulin shock. An adorable miniature Santa with his cutesy reindeer attached to his well-appointed sled stood ready for takeoff at the edge of the coffee table. Various

Santas, elves, and other decorative pictures adorned the walls. The Christmas tree was bare, waiting for my brother, Jack, and I to do the honors. Which we did with cups of cocoa near at hand and mom's eyes twinkling.

She sat regally, her evening drink resting in her grasp, comfortably, like the old friend it was. She glowed at our progress and cheered us on with only an occasional, "Missed a spot," which we would amend with clumps of tinsel and shots of laughter.

God, it was good to be home. I couldn't think why I had dreaded it.

During the whole Greyhound ride across the snowy landscape, my stomach had churned. Cityscapes and rural townships had passed in picturesque glory. Yet I had only smelled the dank odor of bodies crushed into seats, heard the overworked and underpaid—or so he said—driver grumble, and felt the crack in the seat where the ragged plastic rubbed into my jeans.

Now, as Christmas songs played and snow fell in fat flakes, my brother and I decorated the tree, and my mom watched—happiness pooling in her eyes—I wondered at my moodiness. Why was I always so darn glum? Couldn't I just relax and enjoy myself?

So I did. I enjoyed the gift exchange. Early Mass. The open house when mom's friends came and sampled her dark fudge and the variety of snacks we had laid out. I savored every happy smile, every teasing joke, even washing the mountain of dishes in warm, sudsy water. There was a reason for the season, and I knew what it was. Love. Joy. Peace on Earth. Goodwill toward men.

After everything was cleaned and put away, exhaustion hit. I lay in my attic room staring at the blackness, as there was no window to peer through. My first year of teaching had left me bewildered and insecure. Was I really cut out to lead kids to educational enlightenment? So far I hadn't had a whole lot of luck getting anyone to shut up long enough to define the week's spelling words, much less discover the astonishing exploits of early explorers or memorize the time's tables. Who knew that eight-year-olds could get so rowdy? Sheesh. Five months in and my teaching fantasy had cracked under the pressure of thirty-one hyperactive little kids. Didn't take much to make me tumble. But it was a job. That took me away from home.

Why? Mom had been great that year. Life was good. Be happy. I fell asleep convinced that my pep talk had done me good.

Morning came. I knew because the sun rose and nearly blinded me when I went outside to see how much snow had fallen through the night. I stood on the porch, amazed at the beauty of fresh snow spread over the neighborhood. Dressed in white caps, the houses along the street matched like siblings at a family reunion. The expanse of woods in the distance put seasonal greeting cards to shame. Even the university across the street arched its towers and pinnacles in newfound pride at thrusting beyond—not just gross ignorance—but the current weather conditions.

"Katherine!"

I froze. Perhaps not literally but certainly figuratively. The tone, the volume, the acid 'tude told me that Christmas was over even though the season had just begun.

"Come here!"

I didn't need to respond verbally. She knew I would come. She could hear the front door close no matter how softly I pressed the latch into place. She would hear my footsteps, no matter how carefully I tread. She would know, with some kind of extra-sensory freaky-weirdness, when I stood in her doorway.

"Damn you! I said come here. Now!"

Jack had left early. He had only come home for a couple of days. The best days. No fault of his that he had to return to work. Before things got out of hand. Again. He always said that he was older and wiser. He was right.

I faced Mom alone. Well, not entirely alone.

At Mass, I often stared at the lights, the windows, the statues, anywhere but at the tabernacle. Or the altar. The priest swept in and out of my peripheral vision so often, I only noticed the color of his vestments, not his face or form. The vestments rippled deep red.

But that Christmas my eyes had strayed. The golden tabernacle glowed, as if in a spotlight. Must be the sun on the snow, I reasoned. Yet it perplexed me. No slanting rays reached that far. As I sat there, battling my inner demons, I finally settled down and faced the gold box. The house of God. The home of faith. The reason for the season. And for an electrifying moment, I knew that Someone lived inside that box.

"Yes, Mom?"

Her demands were the same as they had been the year before. Her fury spewed forth at the usual rate. She drank and smoked, nearly setting her bed on fire that night. Numbness came to the rescue. As always. Meals prepared. Refused. I took down the decorations. Perhaps to hurry the season along. The tree got sent to the curb. Tinsel froze on the branches.

Sunday afternoon, I took the Greyhound bus back to Chicago.

As I peered out the window, avoiding every possible human encounter, I decided that I just couldn't care anymore. Like every kid who had been lied to, I had struggled for so long to believe that perhaps I had simply misunderstood. That a lie wasn't really a lie. I hadn't been tricked. And heaven and hell weren't the same place.

My appetite had died the moment Mom called my name in *that* tone. Too chicken to kill myself outright, after all, it was a sin to do that, right? I figured I just didn't have to fight to stay alive anymore. I could let death have what despair already prepared, an empty soul.

It was my resolution. Die. As simply and as easily as possible. Before the New Year rolled around, so I wouldn't have to worry about breaking any promises.

In Chicago, I lived in a house with an old woman named Patricia. I paid a meager sum from my meager salary and put medicinal drops in her eyes every night. A fair exchange. She didn't ask much of me. We lived across the street from the church, so she attended social gatherings to her heart's content. She also kept a stack of sultry romances on a chair in her living room.

Considering her advanced years, I found her selection rather astonishing. Apparently, she didn't have any cardiovascular issues.

It was noon when I climbed the steps to her home that she had lived in with her husband of forty years; she had the pictures to prove it. I naturally had to pass through the living room to get to the stairway in order to sneak up to my attic apartment. Painted a sky blue with one window facing north and one south. Not that I could see much more than various roofs and a few stray birds, but it was adequate. And adequate was all I had asked for.

I slipped inside, shut the door ever so softly, quite certain that she'd be napping in her chair and nearly jumped out of my skin when she sprang out from the kitchen like one of those New Year's Eve's poppers that idiots blow in other people's faces. Like that's funny or something?

No matter.

She grinned. A Cheshire cat would've been proud.

"Katherine? You're home!"

I hate it when people state the obvious and then wait. As if they really want confirmation of reality. "Uh. Yeah."

"Oh, good! I just made a sandwich! And I've got a nice glass of cocoa ready! Here! Come in and get warmed up!"

Dang. What was up with all the exclamation marks? Her whole body shivered with the delight of a pen smacking the paper with a dot at the end of an exclaim.

"Uh. No. Thanks. I really appreciate it. But I'm not hungry." No, I didn't tell her the truth. There is no good way to tell an eighty-something-old woman who has survived the demise of her beloved husband, the ravages of breast cancer, the Great Depression, and a World War that I'd given up on life and wanted to starve myself to death as an easy way out.

She shook her head.

What? She couldn't just shake her head and smile at me like that. It wasn't fair. I hated my life. My mom's manic-depressive, schizoid, personality disorder ruined everything. I couldn't hope. I couldn't live and be happy. Life was a damned lie, and that was all there was to it.

"I made grilled tuna with chips!"

In a moment of insane distraction, I actually tried to figure out whether she meant she had grilled the chips with the tuna or if she just screwed with syntax like a possessed Scrabble demon.

Bloody hell but that woman was determined. But so was I. My misery must end. I would not eat another bite of food till...well... Gee. Killing yourself was frowned upon, and I might not get a seat at the Heavenly table. *So what?* I clamped my lips shut.

Then I made a huge mistake. I stood still and let her look at me. Really look. And she saw. Tears formed. All cheer fled. Compassion arrived. And ran me over.

She took my arm and started chatting. A blue jay at the bird feeder filling in all her feathered friends on recent gossip could not have done any better. I hardly noticed when she led me into the warm kitchen and pressed my shoulder hard enough to force my knees to buckle so that I actually sat at the Formica kitchen table. The grilled tuna sat on a plate with little flowers on the border. The chips spilled around the edge. A cup of cocoa sat within easy reach.

"For me?"

It was her question. Not mine. I should have been the one to ask. I should have wondered how she knew I was coming in early. Or why she was fixing me lunch when she never had done so before.

But no. She asked if I would eat to please her. To satisfy some longing she had to watch a miserable, disappointed, despairing woman eat a grilled tuna sandwich at her plastic table.

"Okay."

So I ate the stupid 2000-something calorie meal and watched as she bustled about the kitchen in do-nothing activity that mystified me. I ate every blessed crumb and drank the dregs of the cocoa only slightly surprised that there was a tiny Jesus face on the bottom of the cup.

When I slipped into bed that night, I looked out the window at the sky. Blackness filled the upper echelons of the cityscape, but a few stars twinkled, determined, I guess, not to let the night speak for them.

Christmas was what I had expected, disappointing, yet enthralling nonetheless. Confusion and grief had blanketed my soul. But the light from a golden box spoke of a presence beyond my sight. And an old woman fed me.

I will die someday. But not in despair.

Come Out of the Cold

Originally published on The Writings of A. K. Frailey
12/4/2020

Stupid mistakes left Trix cold. Her own especially. Who on planet Earth was responsible for spelling? And could she find a legal precedent for killing the nameless perpetrators outright, or would it have to be a clandestine affair? Though surely, she'd had a good portion of the world's fifth-graders in her corner.

Was it her fault that few human beings could state her name without topping it off with an "ie," turning her name into a bunny meme, or that gray was spelled with an a on one side of the Atlantic and with an e on the other? What demon-possessed people to care—much less sing-song their way through a quarterly review, insisting that she better shape up or—

The words had been left hanging. Just like that. An unspoken doomsday *"Trix End."*

Trix stomped through the grocery store, huffing through her mask, which only fogged up her glasses. Lord have mercy. Would the trials of the year never end?

Head down, shoulders at ear level, she maneuvered her cart through the seafood aisle, blinking at the prices. She mumbled to herself, though visions of serving shrimp with some-kind-of-undetectable-poison-and-watching-her-bossy-boss-slip-to-the-floor-dead flashed through her mind.

"Hey, *Trixie*!"

Glowing lava rocks exploding from an active volcano had nothing on Trix at that moment. She grimaced, keeping her eyes wide so that as far as anyone reading a masked expression could figure, there was a smile under there somewhere. She faced Brenda, one of the homeschooling moms who sat behind her at Mass. She had polished a small mittened-hand wave to good effect. "Hey, Brenda."

"So, are you going to the Winter Fun Event on the town square on Sunday?"

Rolling her eyes to the ceiling, Trix mentally consulted her calendar. She had to teach school all week, an editing project was due on Thursday, her dad had slipped on the ice, so she wanted to drop off some chocolate panaceas on Friday. Saturday, she'd charge into battle against the encroaching spiderwebs, dust bunnies, and household scum that managed to accumulate when her back was turned. Sunday remained her shield against overwork and flippant insanity. "Well, I'm not sure. I've got a lot going on. And besides, is it safe?"

Attempting to avoid a maniacal expression, Trix hid her grin behind her mask. The "Is it safe?" comment usually stopped every conversation cold. She glanced aside at the rows of frozen foods. A suitable location, indeed.

Even behind her they-all-look-alike mask, it was obvious, Brenda's face fell. Her eyes dimmed. Her joy-spark snuffed.

Geeze! Who cares about Winter Fun? I have my sanity to keep track of! Isn't that more important!

Trix tried to cool the use of mental exclamation points, but her heart sank to her chilled boots. If Old Scrooge could see her now, he'd embrace her as a fellow frozen-soul.

Good soldier and honest Christian lady who kept faith with all sorts of happy thoughts, Brenda squared her shoulders and drowned whatever sorry-reality haunted the depth of her eyes. "No problem. I was just asking. You're right to be careful. Just sometimes, you know—" She glanced aside, definitely not seeing the delightful array of frozen yogurts. "You're doing well. That's all that matters."

Trix's icy heart started to drip.

Her mistake hit Brenda like a bullet train. She burst with contrition. "Oh, I forgot. I said Trixie—and you hate that. Sorry. I mess up names all the time, so I use those stupid mnemonic-things to remember. But I still manage to—" Gripping her cart with dejected humiliation, she aimed for the meat and cheese aisle.

Her cheeks flushed, Trix swallowed a chunk of ice. She stopped Brenda's cart. "I'm heading to the candy aisle to find something chocolatey for my dad. Want to come?"

As they turned into the next aisle and at the sight of Brenda's tear-filled eyes, Trix snatched a box of cocoa off the passing shelf. "You want to stop by for a cup Sunday afternoon? We'll both need warming up." She grinned right through her mask.

It was good to come out of the cold.

The Me I Want to Be

Originally published on The Writings of A. K. Frailey
11/5/2020

Martin, dressed in jeans, a light sweater, and his running shoes, stood on the edge of a gaping hole where his home was supposed to stand and realized that the earth beneath his feet could give way at any time. He stepped back. When the pressure of solid earth penetrated the soles of his feet, he stopped.

Taller than her brother, with long black hair rippling down her back, her body wrapped in a winter coat, yet still shivering, Jacquelyn meandered close and clasped his frozen hand. "You need to forget it. Let it go."

His snort, bitter and abrupt, left no doubt about his feelings on that score. "*It* let me go! It left me without a foundation for my house."

Jacquelyn hugged his arm. Words were of no use now.

With a sigh, he turned away. "There's nothing to do but abandon the whole thing. Chalk it up as a learning experience, though I can't say I learned much. What's a sinkhole supposed to teach me? That my hopes, like my marriage, can drop into the abyss at a moment's notice?"

Jacquelyn pulled a thick strand of hair from her face. "You'll find a better place and another—"

Heat flushed Martin's face as his heartbeat ricocheted through his tense body. "Good God, if you say I'll find another wife, I may never speak to you again."

Tears filled Jacquelyn's eyes.

With an apologetic shake of his head, Martin grabbed her hand and hurried to his truck. "You shouldn't be out here. It's too cold, and you're just getting over that ridiculous flu." He opened the passenger door to his Ford truck and helped her climb in. Then he jogged to the driver's side, slapping his hands to regain feeling in his fingertips. He slid into place, started the car, and backed out of the makeshift driveway.

A few trees still sported burnt orange and yellow leaves. As dark clouds bundled in the west and the wind picked up, only the hardy oaks held fast. The rest would be stripped bare before the week was out. With a sinking feeling, the image of his wife, soon-to-be ex-wife, describing the house she wanted and all the fun they'd have filling it with adorable children, stabbed his gut.

He turned the truck onto the freeway. "You feeling okay?"

Jacquelyn shrugged. "Dad didn't know who I was on my last visit. Jay got laid off, so I'm trying to pick up another online teaching job. Amy hates her biology teacher, and me half the time, but she's getting through. Our family stubborn streak comes in handy." She flashed a smile, though her face didn't reflect it.

His eyes on the road, Martin pressed her arm in a gentle squeeze. "Sorry. I'm not the only one going through stuff." He sighed. "You're right. I got the land cheap, and I'll find another place to build. Sandra only married me for my good looks, charm, and oodles of money. Guess it served her right to discover the frog under her prince, eh?"

Jacquelyn peered out the window, her tears gave way. “She doesn’t know you, or she’d never have left.”

“She knew. She just wanted something else. *Someone* else.”

“She wants *to be* someone else.” Jacquelyn shrugged. “Easy mistake to make.”

Martin took the right lane and followed it to the exit. He curved with the road, checked the quiet intersection, and pulled onto Main Street. Going a modest 30 mph felt like crawling.

A group outside the Famished Farmers café waved as they passed.

Martin waved back.

Jacquelyn imitated an Egyptian mummy.

With a tilt of his head, Martin frowned. “Wasn’t that blond with the spike heels your friend from—?”

“She made some comments on my peer review...pretty harsh. I’m staying out of her way.”

“Oh.”

“Her husband had a crush on me and well...”

Martin winced. *God, when did life get so bloody complicated?*

As he wound his way through town, Martin picked a safe topic. “Still taking your medicine?”

“Only if I have trouble breathing. Been doing well the last few days.” She glanced aside. “And you? Still taking that anti-depressant?”

Martin wanted to slam his head against the steering wheel as he picked up speed along the country road. “No. I had lots of reasons to be depressed, but it isn’t the end of the world. I just need to figure out how to get undepressed.”

A hound chasing a rabbit dashed out in front of the truck.

Martin swerved, hit the brakes, and skidded to abrupt stop inches from a deep ravine.

As they sat there, stunned, Jacquelyn exhaled a long shuddering breath.

Martin swiveled out of the truck, not even bothering to slam the door shut. He strode around, stared at the tires peeking over the edge of the gorge, and waved at his sister. "Don't move!"

He sped to the truck, slipped into place, and slowly edged the car backward. Then he started to sob.

Jacquelyn rubbed his back in a large, slow circle. "Catch your breath, Marty."

Martin rested his head on the steering wheel. "After the accident, I thought I'd be strong. Mom died so quick. But no matter what I do, Dad's slipping into senility. Despite the fact that my wife found a guy she likes better, I still planned to build the house, and then the ground sinks from under me, literally. And now, I nearly drive us off a cliff." Martin lifted his head and stared at his sister. "You think someone got me mixed up with a guy named Job?"

A tired smile ghosted across Jacquelyn's face. "Life is hellishly hard, but we hang in there anyway."

Martin's mind drew a blank. "Why? It'd be so much easier to give up."

Jacquelyn dug into her purse and pulled out a wallet. She snapped open a small picture album and wiggled out a photo. It was a long-legged, longer-haired Martin, age twelve. She held it up.

Martin leaned forward; his jaw dropped open. "What're you doing carrying that around? It should be burned! I'm wearing bell-bottoms, for Heaven's sake! It could be used against me in a court of law."

Jacquelyn snatched it back and pressed it to her chest. "It's mine. When I have a bad day, I pull it out."

Martin shook his head, confusion rising like late-summer fog.

"This was the year that guy I loved dumped me for my best friend, I got that awful perm, and I failed algebra. Mom was working evenings, Dad started drinking, and I hated everyone."

"You were fifteen." He pointed to the picture. "Why are—"

"You took me out for ice cream, and I punched you, splattering chocolate sauce on your good shirt. Made a big stain on the front, you can still see the mark." She tapped the picture.

A smile spread across his face, reaching his heart. "You were a bully. What's new?"

"I tried to apologize by ordering you to wear a clean shirt, but you said that you'd know people by what they saw. Either they'd see a stain or they'd see you. Later you gave the shirt to Rosco so he'd sleep in the doghouse without barking all night."

Martin ran his fingers through his hair. "Color me confused."

"When I look at the picture, I see the me I want to be. I don't see a stain. I see possibilities."

Martin tilted his head, put the car into gear, and pulled onto the road. "You think I could turn a sinkhole into a basement or something?"

Jacquelyn laughed. “Make it a family room, and I’ll help you build it.”

Martin dropped Jacquelyn at home and then headed to the worksite. He was back on solid ground.

Ever My Intention

Originally published on The Writings of A. K. Frailey
10/9/2020

Samantha Keller just wanted to find a toothbrush. That's all she asked out of life. Not an unreasonable request. Not considering the fact that she had just bitten into a luscious, though thoroughly deceptive, apple from her neighbor's tree, which had seconds before been home to a fat worm. Her frantic attempt at brushing her teeth in a hurry resulted in the toothbrush flipping between her fingers and landing in the toilet.

Hovering in front of the bathroom closet, patting the shelf just above her eye level where she always put the extras, availed nothing but sticky fingers. An empty cough syrup bottle lay like a forgotten soldier on a battlefield before red goo seepage and a decidedly sick-pink cotton ball offering testimony of other clumsy encounters.

Life really shouldn't be this hard.

"Oh, to heck with it." She turned to the sink, popped open the mouthwash, did a complete rinse, and considered herself lucky.

She peered into the mirror and saw her mom's face. Though her hair sported the salt and pepper look of a middle-aged woman who can't decide if she's a new 40 or an old 50, the trapped expression of her mother riveted her gaze to the glass. "Ba-ba-ba..." Like a nursery rhyme never finished, Mom couldn't get her words out, though her eyes pleaded for understanding.

Samantha yanked herself away and refocused. She tromped down the hall to the kitchen and stared at the bowl brimful of beautiful apples. “Tricked me once but not twice.” She snatched the paring knife off the counter.

The phone rang. She checked. A local number.

She answered with all the confidence of a homeowner in good standing, whose neighborhood friends might check on her once in a blue moon. “Hello?”

“As a residential customer, we would like you to answer a few simple—”

Slapping the end button, Samantha frowned. She had answered four scam calls through the week and vowed to let it ring forevermore. If someone wanted to actually talk with her, they’d leave a message, right? Why on Earth did she keep falling for the latest in life’s tricks?

Reaching for the knife, the phone rang again. With a shrug, she insisted on outwitting the maniacal scammers who poured out their lives in demolishing humanity’s trust in the phone system.

It stopped ringing.

She plucked an apple from the mound and made the first cut.

The phone rang again.

Completely against her will, Samantha glanced at the glowing screen and recognized the number. Her sister in Wisconsin. Blanch and her husband ran a dairy farm south of the city and made a decent living while raising the cutest set of twins God ever created.

Rolling every ounce of ill humor off her shoulders and sliding onto a stool, she leaned against the counter and let the apple and the knife fall from her fingers. "Hey, Blanch! I was just thinking of you while—"

A sob choked the line.

Samantha lifted the phone from her ear and stared at it. Had she lost the connection? Another scammer copying her sister's number?

Sobbing tumbled into crashing thunder. A wail screeched over four hundred miles and smacked Samantha in the face.

"Oh, God, Blanch! What—?"

"She's dead! I can't believe it!"

Agony shivered over Samantha as tears sprang to her eyes. "Dead? Who?"

"Mom! She died during the night. I stopped by early to give her some homemade cookies and fresh apples off our tree, but when the nurse went to check on her..." Sobbing rampaged over a cliff.

Tired truisms sprang to Samantha's lips. *It's better this way...a blessed relief...Mom would want us to live on...to celebrate her life without all the horrific dementia...*

But no words came.

They weren't truly true. Not yet, anyway.

As tears meandered down her cheeks, her husband Elliott wandered into the room. He frowned at her tears, bent low, and took her hand.

She listened to Samantha's cascading grief, dragged a notepaper and pen front and center and wrote, "Mom died," and shoved the bald announcement toward her husband.

Wrapping a comforting arm around her shaking shoulders, he offered what he could, a gentle murmur of sorrow.

A week later...

Samantha faced the mound of dirt piled in front of her parents' headstone. Mom's nicely dressed body lay four and a half feet under, safely encased in a mahogany coffin inside a cement vault, right next to her dad's resting place. Samantha's gaze wandered over the birthdates and death dates, and the scripture quote, "You shall be known by your fruit." The etching of two apple trees that her mother had insisted mark their last place on earth stood in testimony to lives that never stopped bearing love and goodness even when they couldn't say a word.

Elliott edged closer.

Her son, daughter, sister, various friends, and relations had come to the funeral and left shortly after. Samantha had returned for three days in a row, trying to understand how something as luscious as life could hold such a worm as death.

Elliott took her hand and said nothing. Wonderful in the mystery of communal silence, he didn't need to fix her grief. He simply shared it.

Autumn leaves swirled from the colorful trees as black crows perched on mossy gravestones, creating a scene Alfred Hitchcock would've been proud to call his own.

"She was a beautiful baby." Samantha had spent hours reviewing old family photos the night before, sharing her favorites with her patient husband.

Elliott smiled. "She was a good and holy woman with a gentle heart."

"Though she could be a stickler! Remember how she insisted that every Thanksgiving had to be celebrated at her house?"

Elliot nodded.

"And she never did forgive Dad. She held his mistakes up to the light of day every chance she got. Trying to drag him to Heaven, she'd say, but it made life miserable sometimes."

Elliott bowed his head.

The cell phone rang.

Samantha pulled it from her coat pocket.

Blanch.

After hitting the talk button, Samantha strolled across the graveyard toward a cluster of trees. "Yes, honey?"

Blanch's voice rose strong and clear. "Just checking in. I made a pie for the kids and thought of Mom. I just wanted to hear your voice."

Samantha stared at the tree in front of her. "Were there any worms in it?"

"Worms? In what?"

"The pie." Samantha cleared her voice and tried to jiggle her brain into coherent thought. "I bit into an apple the other day...and you know..."

A chuckle broke the silence. "Oh, no. The pie looks delicious." Her voice took on mom's imperious tone. "You're supposed to cut the worms out before you eat the fruit, you know."

Ever my intention.

Samantha took her husband's hand, meandered to the car, and left the mound of dirt behind.

You Know It's Real

Originally published on The Writings of A. K. Frailey
9/25/2020

Patrick O'Donnell had been married for eighteen years, and only today did he realize that he loved his wife.

Emily had insisted on an October wedding, though he knew that was ridiculous. Couldn't trust the weather in October any better than a used car on the highway. Still, rather than listen to her complain every anniversary about how she wished she had gotten to pick the date, he had acquiesced.

He sat in their bedroom and rubbed his stubbly chin. At fifty-two, he was a relatively strong and good-looking guy. Any woman would be lucky to have him, even now. He certainly got inquiring looks when he was away from home. He'd made a habit of placing his left hand, thus his "owners tag," in plain sight so whomever he was interviewing would get the hint, and there'd be no awkward moments. Flattered by the shine in a woman's eyes, he enjoyed knowing that he still attracted women, but he rarely let it go for long before he'd make some obvious comment about his wife and kids, clarifying his position.

Only once did he joke with Em about his magnetic power with women. She didn't see the humor. She took it like a challenge. The next time they went out, she flirted with every guy in the room, and every time they grinned at her, she sent a beaming smile his way.

He'd come to marriage late in life, and at thirty-four, his mom had all but given up hope for him. He didn't date much since the whole asking out and wading through the get-to-know-you process disturbed him.

Emily was a schoolteacher seven years his junior when they met. He was a reporter for the city paper. When he did a piece about their accelerated school program, she was one of the people he interviewed. In fact, he interviewed her three times before he asked her out.

It wasn't long before he asked her to marry him.

After a church wedding, one of the few times he went to church, he traveled for the paper, wrote articles, took a series of editing positions, did freelance work, studied photography, took yearly wilderness trips with the guys, even did a stint in Guatemala for six weeks one summer.

Emily did much the same, living life to the fullest.

Patrick rose from the edge of the bed and faced the open French doors blowing in a gentle breeze. The last day of September. Tomorrow was October first and their eighteenth anniversary. But for the first time in their married life, Emily wouldn't care.

The process had started so slowly that neither of them thought that anything was wrong. Just an occasional headache. Then the slight trembling. When she couldn't remember how to get to the grocery store, she had laughed it away. "Too much on my mind, what with violence on the rise, and three kids failing my class. Lucky I can remember my name!"

It seemed mildly amusing, until it wasn't.

Footsteps padded near. *Bare feet by the sound of it.* Patrick shook his head. His kids befuddled him. Clare was the more logical of the two, but Tige was easier to handle. Clare had a knack for misunderstanding him while Tige didn't seem to care. As long as he could see his friends and play games on a regular basis, he'd do whatever his parents asked. A fair trade, he'd say. But Clare classified and parsed everything. Big jobs required big rewards. He asked as little as possible from her.

"Hey, Dad?" Tall and lanky at sixteen, Tige stood in the doorway in his baggy black sweatpants and long-sleeved shirt, a set he used as his nightclothes for the last year.

Patrick returned his gaze to the outdoors. The sun had risen but with the heavy mist, a dreary gray hung over the land. He could barely make out the neighbor's house just beyond the two maple trees.

"Yeah?"

Tige stepped in and stopped just behind Patrick's right elbow. "Just thinking that Mom'd like it if we did something tomorrow. Maybe we could bring her flowers. There're a few blooms left on the Rose of Sharon."

A choking ache rose from the depth of his being and flooded Patrick's whole body. The porch railing blurred.

A higher voice rose from behind. Clare, petite with long blond hair and bright blue eyes, so much like her mother, took charge. "Those'll wilt before we get there. The cafeteria lady owns a shop that sells decorative arrangements, fake ones that won't fade. I could get some after school since it's Friday, and I don't have to get my school work done in a hurry."

Annoyance squeezed Patrick's heart, but he couldn't say anything. She was right. Fresh flowers, even colorful leaves, would fade and look terrible in a few days. But still—

"Mom hates fake stuff, Clare. We aren't doing this to save you trouble. We're doing what mom loved best."

A tear meandered down Patrick's cheek. He knew who else loved Emily.

Her voice high and strained, Clare ground her point into their hearts. "Mom won't know the difference."

Patrick turned around. "We will." He clasped his son's shoulder. "Pick a few just before we leave in the morning. It won't matter how they look in a week."

Tige nodded and padded out the door.

Clare's mouth trembled. "Why not get something that lasts? It'll look better when she wakes up—"

Patrick held out his arms. No words could explain.

Clare flung herself into her dad's embrace and held on for dear life.

After the room was clear, the fog had lifted, and the clock insisted that he get ready for work, Patrick closed the French doors.

Love hurts like hell, he realized. He wiped his eyes and faced the day. Maybe that's when you know it's real.

Mostly I Live Life

Originally published on The Writings of A. K. Frailey
9/11/2020

Rebah stared—turning her head as far back as it would go—at the crow perched on an old wooden post in front of rows of golden corn stalks, as she drove no less than sixty on the rural Illinois road.

She should've stopped. By the time she made up her mind and looked in the rearview mirror, the proud plumage was flying high across the cornfield into the bean field.

Where're you going?

It couldn't hear her and wouldn't care to answer if it did. Rebah only wanted to stare at it long enough to imbibe the magical power it held—the mystical passion embodied in a carefree moment.

She glanced at her handbag leaning forlornly on the passenger seat, the strap folded across the open pocket that held the keys to her current existence—her cell phone and her to-do list.

Jed, she repeated. *Jed. Not Jeb or Jacob. It's Jed.* She tried to picture the man her husband, Brad, told her owned the shop.

"Tall, lanky, elderly guy with gray hair."

Gee, thanks, Honey. Got it now.

Rebah stretched her mind back. Had Brad ever used figurative language? Did he ever describe a person as more than a combination of physical attributes? It was one of the things she'd loved about him—his honest, clear thinking. Never sarcastic like her dad or manipulative like her sister. Just a straightforward kind of man.

Three plump blackbirds stood at odd angles to each other on the road ahead. Apparently, they weren't in a hurry, but she was. As her car zoomed up to the twenty-yard mark, they flapped into the blue September sky, majestic and unperturbed. "We're heading on anyway, Lady. Don't think for a second that you altered our plans."

She wanted to laugh. Giggle. A smirk would do. But she had to find Jed's countryside shop and buy a part for the mower. It was an old mower and needed an old part, preferably one that worked. It was all Greek to her. Mowers belonged in the same category as electricity and nuclear fusion.

A right on Acorn Road, two streets down, and on the left, 119 E. Acorn Rd., a workshop appeared as if by magic. A wooden structure built back and to the left of a cottage that belonged in a land of "far away and long ago." Charming hardly described it.

The rock driveway lined with late-season flowers curved around the back of the shop. She parked, rolled down the window, and imbibed.

The porch cozied over two garden beds run riot with daisies, asters, chrysanthemums, and coneflowers. Cornstalks tied to the railings decorated the steps as a scarecrow stood watch, both his smile and his pitchfork ready for service. Hanging plants perked up the mellow season with dashes of red and green, while ceramic squirrels scampered down the steps, leading to a maple tree just breaking into full autumn glory.

Rebah climbed out of her car and exhaled. "Good God in heaven!"

"Yeah, I'd say that's about right."

The man's deep voice followed by a light chuckle turned Rebah's gaze.

Coming from the dim interior of the shop, ambled a man exactly as her husband described. Except her husband had failed to mention the bulbous nose, oversized ears, long gray beard, and the sweetest eyes she had ever delved.

"What can I do for you?"

Rebah wondered if she was in love. She wanted to live in this little house, sit on a bench, watch this gentle giant work in his shop, and absorb the conviviality that emanated from the air in this enchanted spot on Acorn Road.

She spluttered, "Oh, yes, actually, my-uh, husband sent me over to get a part. Brad. My husband. He needs something you have."

She wasn't sure if that last part was a question or a statement of fact, but she prayed Jed was a mind reader since she could no longer rely on the power of speech.

"Brad? Oh, yes!" Jed grinned impishly as befitted the gnome-spirit he represented. "I have the part right here in my shop. I was just cleaning it a bit. They get a mite dusty sitting on the shelf, don't you know."

A howl of laughter fought earnestly with a sob of despair. By all the saints, Rebah knew about dust! Dust bunnies and spider webs had beaten her into submission long ago. Who on earth cleaned an engine part? A pitiful squeak was the best she could manage as the battle ended in a draw.

"Well, come on in and have a cup of something while you wait. I like a little spiced cider as the evening draws close. Perks a fellow up after a long day." He ambled back into the shop, turning a switch on the wall just inside the doorway.

Yellow lamplight flooded the room, conjuring images of children's fairytale books. Cherry-stained shelves lined the walls, filled with an impossible variety of projects. Small engine parts, kitchen essentials—toasters and mixers, a variety of wall clocks, one small organ, two violins, and, of course, an assortment of broken toys stood, sat, or leaned in repose for their appointment with Jed's dexterous fingers.

Rebah tried to shake herself into conscious reality. "So, you're a fixer? A repair guy?" Oh heck, that seemed as inadequate as calling a CIA agent a sleuth.

After pouring a fresh cup of cider into a mug from a dark brown jug and setting it within easy reach, Jed ran a cloth lovingly over the metal part that—in Rebah's opinion—hardly deserved the attention.

She sipped the cider, warmth tingling all over. Her eyes strayed to the mower part. She frowned. It was just metal, after all. It would go in a machine, get dirty again, and no one would care in the least.

"I fix those things that I can. Mostly, I live life."

A lump formed in Rebah's throat. She blinked.

Two crows and three blackbirds hopped up to the open doorway, their bright eyes keeping a careful watch on Rebah.

Jed laughed. He laid the metal part on his workbench, scooped an old can into a plump bag hanging on the wall, then carried the full container of seeds to the doorway. He scattered supper to the hungry throng and watched them in serene joy.

Rebah watched his every move as absorbed as it was the finale of her favorite primetime drama. "God, I want what you've got."

It felt like cold water in the face when Rebah realized that she had said the words out loud.

"Eh?" Jed returned to his machine part. He wrapped it in a clean cloth and laid it at the bottom of a paper bag. He folded the bag neatly and handed it to Rebah.

She slurped the rest of her drink, letting the warm tingly feeling bring a smile to her face, covering her confusion. Perhaps he hadn't heard. "How much do I owe you?"

"Ten ought to cover it. It's a recycled part and didn't need much mending."

She ran to her car, dropped the bag on the back seat, shuffled through her purse, found two fives, scurried back, and met Jed in front of his porch steps. She handed him the money. A longing nearly broke her heart. "I wish my place looked like this. More, I wish I felt like...this...place."

To Rebah's astonishment, Jed smiled.

"Yeah. That's how I was when I first came here. I'd been in the army for more years than I can remember, fought people I didn't want to fight, lost family to drugs and alcohol, though my youngest sister died of cancer last year. But you know, the old woman who owned this place said that it just needed tender care. If I'd give it that and do every task with gentle love, I'd be repaid in full." Jed tapped the railing. "By golly, she wasn't off the mark."

Tears filled Rebah's eyes. "You don't mean that my place could look like this?"

"No. This place belongs here on Acorn Road. But the beauty I wake up to every day? Why, that belongs everywhere that'll allow it in."

~~~

When Rebah drove up to her short straight driveway, her husband stood on their overgrown lawn, grinning.

She grinned back. "I've got the part, and I'll get dinner on in a minute, Love."

When a crow flapped overhead, she knew whom she'd invite to dinner next.
~~~

Between the Raindrops

Originally published on The Writings of A. K. Frailey
8/14/2020

Saundra realized that running between the raindrops, like so many things in life, wasn't meant to be taken literally. So why was she scurrying madly to her neighbor's house with any expectation that she would be dry when she got there?

Bradley stared hard as she leaped over the threshold into the open living room-kitchen of their ranch-style house.

"An umbrella was out of the question, huh?"

Saundra didn't deem it necessary to reply. She knew why she'd come, and it outweighed mere comfort. She couldn't look Bradley in the eye.

A woman's voice screeched from the top of the stairs. "Hey! Kiddos, get ready for bed now, or Sandy won't read you a story."

The collective sighing, whimpering, and bickering over who got to pick out the first story plucked Saundra's raw nerves. Who did she think she was? Superwoman coming to the rescue?

She peeled off her soggy shoes and figured that one evening in damp socks wouldn't kill her. The kids might. But that was merely theoretical.

Anne tottered down the stairs on skyscraper heels, wearing a tight-fitting, burgundy dress that clearly hadn't been outside the closet in years. Once landed, she tinkered with her earrings and shot a glance at her husband. "Get up there and make them behave."

An eye roll clarified Bradley's lack of enthusiasm for the assignment as he mounted the steps.

The initial plea-bargaining Anne used when asking for one night out with her husband without the kids had merely sent a flicker of anxiety through Saundra's evening plans. No big deal. The kids were a little rambunctious Anne had said but easier than her nephews. Of course, Godzilla was easier than the aforementioned nephews.

A little girl's scream, a man's barking order, serious commotion, two slamming doors, pounding footsteps, and Bradley's flushed face glowering at his wife made Saundra reconsider her assessment. Maybe Godzilla would be easier. After all, there was only one of him.

Anne snatched a lavender purse off a scratched end table and charged for the door. "They'll settle down. Just let them cool off and read a story with milk and cookies before bed."

Bradley jerked his car keys around like he'd prefer to catapult them rather than put them to their rightful purpose.

The thought, *Get drunk fast*, shot through Saundra's mind. She nodded at Anne's retreating back, dumbfounded.

It wasn't until the Ford Explorer squealed into the night that she realized that the kids didn't even know her. And she didn't know them.

A little girl's voice called from the tops of the steps—Sandy?

~~~
~~~

The milk and cookies were easy to locate.

Five-year-old Jimmy had a future in mountain climbing the way he scaled the kitchen counter, scrambled to the cabinet over the refrigerator, plucked the hidden cookies from the depths, (next to the chardonnay), and leaped to the floor with his prize.

Jan, at the cultivated age of seven, demurely retrieved three short glasses, lugged the gallon of milk to the table, and sportingly poured everyone a full glass.

Remarkably, a story compromise was reached on relatively benign terms. Each child picked out a short story, and Saundra got to pick a long one. After teeth had been brushed, the kids joined their sitter on the couch and curled up one on each side.

Their body warmth, light patter of rain, and the yellow lamplight settled Saundra's nerves into a state of peaceful repose. Books made for an evening of simple pleasure. Every Friday afternoon, she read a short story out loud to her high school class. They always groaned the first time. They never groaned the second.

She cracked open the first book and climbed inside. Along with the kids.

By the time the clock chimed midnight, Saundra wondered if she should call the police. After *The Velveteen Rabbit*, the kids had gone to bed quietly. She shuddered through the late news, and the rain had quit hours ago. She stretched out on the couch fully aware that she'd fall asleep within seconds.

Before her eyes closed, a door was thrust open and keys slammed on the counter, jolting her nerves wide awake. Loud voices. Slurred speech. Hard-soled shoes pounding up the steps.

Saundra's first instinct was to quiet the two down before they woke the kids. But the realization that this was their house shushed her mouth.

"Sandy? Where'd you get to, girl?"

Sandy rose and stepped into the kitchen.

Anne's smeared eyeliner, drooping lower lip, and glassy stare froze Saundra in place.

"There you are. Thought maybe you'd abandoned me."

"I'd never do that."

Water ran. Bradley's heavy tread crossed the room above.

Saundra frowned as she glanced up. "The kids are asleep."

"Sure. You did great." She dropped her purse on the counter. "Mind if I pay you in the morning? I doubt my writing's too clear right now."

Slipping on her damp shoes, Saundra sucked in a deep breath. She wanted the quiet peaceful time with the kids cuddled on each side of her, listening with bated breath, their eyes glued to the illustrated page. Sharing their love of a good story, life itself.

A lump rose in her throat, and words got stuck on the way out. "You two have a good time?"

Anne shrugged. "We drank and talked about the garbage in our lives." Kicking off her shoes, she lost balance and had to grip the counter. "Piss poor world we live in. Kids will hate us when they grow up. Might hate us now, for all I know."

Tears threatened. Saundra turned the door handle. "They don't hate anyone. Yet."

A star-filled sky accompanied Saundra home. The smell of late summer rain, wet earth, a faint rose scent lifted her spirits. She could hear Jan's voice pleading, see Jimmy's dark eyes imploring. "Will you come again and read to us?"

She would. She'd even run between the raindrops if she had to.

Hope for the Human Race

Originally published on The Writings of A. K. Frailey
7/17/2020

Herman perched his glasses on his nose, stared at the bottle of bathroom cleaner with the foamy suds on the label, and swerved his gaze to his beloved dog—the one giving him the mopey *What-did-I-Do-To-Deserve-This?* look—and realized his mistake.

It wasn't the first time.

The week before, he had brushed his teeth with Icy-Hot, and the week before that, he had poured half a bottle of liquid detergent down the drain thinking he was unclogging the sink. The fact that the dishes had smelled "springtime fresh" hadn't helped in the least. The sink remained clogged until the plumber sent his snake coil five miles through underground terrain.

Each morning, when the news informed him that a new plague or disasters unlimited loomed, he figured that this was as good a time as any to make out a will. Dying was all too easy. It was living that made each day a challenge.

And so, when he met Chuck, he tried not to act surprised. Chuck looked perfect. He acted perfect. Up until the moment he froze in place. That wasn't so perfect. Not the way he did it. Stock still. His hand caught in mid-air, holding the test tube just so. His eyes staring, blank, but as wide and as blue as ever.

After the last major world alteration—pandemic, economic crisis, collective emotional meltdown—whatever you want to call it, The University had decided that "State of the Art Androids" would assist human teachers in their laboratory work. No matter if the world was going to hell-in-a-hand-basket, students still needed the opportunity to practice medical procedures, carry out chemical experiments, and do a thousand things that simply could not be managed from home.

Reasonable? Of course.

Considering his record of late, Herman wasn't surprised when his Department Head informed him that a new assistant, Chuck, would aide him as he maneuvered the entire scientific student body through the semester. To stiffen his spine, Herman reminded himself that his dog had recovered nicely and water ran through his sink lickity-split these days, with a refreshing scent to boot.

He spent the entire weekend before Chuck's arrival assuring himself that an assistant meant more free time to do his own research. A positive step in the right direction. An honor! And *NO* risk.

When autumn rolled around and the school doors finally creaked open, Chuck calculated formulas, measured chemicals, laid out lab materials, and never broke anything. Never got mixed up. Never forgot which student he was dealing with or which experiment they were doing. Though his pronunciation did need a little work. Good thing scientists rarely giggle.

But last Wednesday, Chuck had a few internal issues, not gastric of course, just something a little off. He bumped Herman twice as they crossed paths in the lab, and he actually scowled at Lacy, the brightest student in the whole school, who had the unfortunate luck to break her arm. Chuck didn't slow down for bumbling humans and didn't smile at imperfections.

Lacy's attempt at humor as she held up her sling-shod arm collided with Chuck's long, cold stare.

Herman glanced at Lacy; tears filled her eyes.

He had suspected for months that her heart had been beating a little faster whenever Chuck was in the room...but this kind of workplace awkwardness he had never imagined. Made soaping the dog with the wrong kind of suds seem almost funny.

What to do? It wasn't like he could call Herman out for his icy demeanor, his lack of empathy, his calculated perfection.

But on Friday, Chuck stalled. Positively and undeniably froze in place.

Herman called the proper authorities. Nodded sympathetically when the Head of the Department broke down sobbing. Chuck had been a prototype. "A first, damn it! But not the last!" The Head Man had lifted his chin and had thrown a determined glare directly at Lacy. As if her human indelicacy had pushed Chuck's tightly wound synaptic system over the proverbial cliff.

After two men with a squeaky dolly wheeled Chuck away, Herman shrugged and considered the lab. Test tubes, beakers, Bunsen burners, metal trays, and laptops—various tools of the trade—and one lonely shrub decorated the sterile white room.

A crash and Herman knew in his heart-of-hearts that there was one less test tube.

He blinked at Lacy. A tear slid down her face.

He padded softly to her side and wrapped his arm around her shoulder.

She leaned in and sighed. “I can’t help it. I make mistakes.”

For the first time in months, Herman felt hope for the human race.

With or Without the Pits

Originally published on The Writings of A. K. Frailey
7/3/2020

Eugene closed the oven door and faced his wife. "I hope I got all the pits out, or the boys will break their teeth on my cherry tarts."

Samantha didn't smile.

It was pouring rain and though the weather forecaster hadn't suggested building an ark, her longed-for vacation at the lake seemed like a fading vision. A swampy muck of floodwaters hardly encouraged suntan-by-the-shore-eat-drink-and-dance-dreams.

With his hands on her shoulders, Eugene tried for a half-caress-half-shake. "I was only kidding. No deep metaphor of the state of the universe."

Like a rusty robot, Samantha rotated to the French doors off the kitchen. The hanging plants sparkled with raindrops while a pair of red slippers she'd left by her favorite chair appeared as droopy as her spirits. "Summer will end, and I'll be as exhausted as ever."

Eugene didn't know what to say. Cherry tarts seemed inconsequential. Like war humor—it just wouldn't work as planned. Some things weren't funny.

Devon, their six-foot-three and two-hundred-pound son, loomed into the room. His shadow entered first. He stopped, glanced from one parent to the next, and then shuffled his feet—indecision warring with better judgment. "Hey, just to let you know, I got the job. They want me to start next week. So—"

Though his heart soared with pride, Eugene's stomach plummeted. Not for a minute could he glance at his wife and deal with her emotional mash-up. No, he'd go it alone. He threw his arms wide and embarrassed the hell out of his eldest with the tightest bear hug he'd given since Devon fell out of the treehouse at four and managed to walk away unscathed.

Doing a darn good impression of a startled linebacker with no ball in sight, Devon let himself be hugged. Then he hugged back.

Samantha stayed on the sidelines. Silent. Stoic. It took a full two and a half minutes before her composure crumbled, and she charged into the hug. Her muffled, "I can't believe you'll be leaving us...I'm so proud, but I can't believe..." reverberated against the men's You-Know-What-I-Mean eye lock.

Eugene pulled back and sniffed, fear reverberating through his body. "The tarts!" A quick U-turn.

Samantha tossed him the oven mitts.

Their youngest son, Kris sauntered in with the grace of a gangling teen that has outgrown every bit of his summer clothing. "Hey! You hear about Devon?" His gaze shifted from his mom to his brother. "I'll get your room, right? It's bigger than mine, and besides, you can sleep on the couch if you ever come to visit."

Samantha slapped her little boy's arm and pooh-pooed the very idea. "Wait till he's out of the house before any formal takeover." She leaned in and stage-whispered. "I have a whole house re-do that'll cost a fortune, and I don't want your dad to suffer cardiac arrest before I get a good contractor set up."

Eugene waved a succulent, cherry popover before his wife's face. "No goodies until you behave."

Lightning flashed and thunder rolled over the celestial landscape.

Not to be held back by the threat of burned fingers or tongue, Kris attacked the hot cookie tray with the gusto of a starved rhinoceros.

Devon lowered his gaze.

Samantha accepted her husband's offering and held it out to her eldest. "You first, Sweetie. The man of the hour."

Eugene wrapped his arm around his wife, and together they watched their sons partake of his latest culinary delight. He tipped his head, touching hers. "So the lake is out—but a cave tour would be pretty cool. Literally and figuratively."

Samantha shrugged, her gaze wandering the room and out the door. Soothing drops fell in a steady rhythm while the fields and trees glowed, revitalized. "After we see Devon off…No hurry."

While Eugene scrubbed the cookie trays, his wife chatted on the phone, spreading good news along the family gossip chain. A send-off party with matching luggage was in the works.

Once he slid the trays into place, Eugene eyed the last popover. He hadn't even had one yet. He refilled his coffee cup, pulled out a chair, and plunked down for a well-earned respite. He took a bite. Wow! Better than he realized. He chewed and savored and finally licked the last crumbs from his fingers. Not one pit.

With a sigh of contentment, he returned to the sink, washed his cup, and reset the coffee machine. He poured the spent grounds into the compost container and froze. There was Devon's napkin with the red insignia of his new company—his mom had forgotten which job he had applied for. There, on the napkin, lay a cherry pit.

The silent accusation stared at him. He hadn't gotten them all. Devon had never said a word. Eugene glanced at his wife. Did she know?

Samantha caught his gaze and frowned.

What should he do? Pretend it didn't exist?

Samantha hung up and sauntered over. Wrapping her arm around her husband, she nuzzled his neck. "Say, how about we celebrate our successful launching of son number one into the world tonight?"

Eugene held up the cherry pit pinched in his fingers. "I missed one." Blinking back ridiculous tears, he fought the hammer blows pummeling his heart. "He could've broken his tooth and then—"

Samantha nudged her husband aside and practically sat in his lap, her arm still around his neck. "There are always cherry pits, honey. We'll never get them all. Or stop rainy-day blues. Some things aren't possible."

Eugene nodded. She was right. But still, his heart ached. Damn cherry pit.

Footsteps approached, and Samantha practically fell on the floor in her haste to get on her feet. She stroked her husband's cheek and then patted Devon's arm as she headed out of the room.

Devon leaned in the kitchen doorway. "Hey, dad, before I go...just wondering..."

Eugene climbed to his feet and met his son's bashful gaze. "Yeah?"

"Could you give me the recipe for your cherry tarts?"

Eugene smiled. He didn't have to ask if his son wanted them with or without the pits.

They both knew.

The Wheel or the Ball

Originally published on The Writings of A. K. Frailey
6/19/2020

"This town is teeming with eligible bachelors. If you're looking for love in all the wrong places."

Cindy nodded, though her gaze stayed fixed on the hamster cage. She hadn't honestly been listening. Of far more universal importance was whether Fred was sleeping...or...Gasp! Quite dead. There was no way on earth that her little girl was going to buy the I-don't-know-what-happened—he-just-died excuse. Though the truth remained, Cindy really didn't know what had happened. Heck. He was a rodent, after all. Rodents don't live forever. Just seems like it when you're a parent.

Jan stomped over, bent low, and added her gaze to the scene. "What are we looking at?"

Fred emerged from his wood-shaving encrusted boudoir. His whiskers twitching and his beady black eyes sparkling with a mischievous "Thought I was a goner, did ya?" expression.

Cindy sighed. Extravagantly. The munchkin drama wasn't quite over. This tamed vermin would haunt her nights running the wobbly wheel of life a little longer. Oh well. He was rather cute for a critter with no tail and an independent personality.

She glanced at her desk. The jury duty summons sat next to her computer, which edged a stack of notebooks arranged for her convenience. She ignored them in order of importance. At the bottom her house repair list. On top sat a list of dinner options. Grilled tuna and cheese sounded amazingly good right now.

"So, are we going out or what?"

"I've done my shopping, and church isn't till Sunday. I'm not sure what going out would accomplish at this point."

Eye roll. Jan had mastered it to a scintillating art form. "Just get out of the house, see something different. Maybe meet some new people. You know. Live-a-little." Jan's bug-eyed expression conveyed the theory that living involved effort beyond breathing and sustaining life functions.

Cindy begged to differ. "I'm still working on my lesson plans for next week, and the hens have taken up squatting rights in the garage. It's time I gave them due notice."

Thigh slap accompanied by yet another eye roll. Jan had it down. "Woman! You are so boring. All you ever do is work."

Perhaps a change of location would ricochet the conversation into the outer atmosphere. Cindy swiped her muffin recipe book under her arm and charged into the kitchen. It was only two in the afternoon, and Patrick and Kelly loved muffins. Why not make them happy? Why not tilt the whole universe toward muffin-induced-joy?

The fact that the baking tins slammed on the counter like bullets discharged from a WWII blunderbuss did nothing to deter Jan's train of thought. "We never have any fun!"

Apparently whining didn't stop when one reached middle age.

Jan plopped down on the kitchen stool and propped her head on her hands. A picture of disconsolate teetering on the edge of depression. "I'm divorced, and you're a widow. Men are a pain in the...well...you know, but we can't live without them. Well, we can, but we'd rather not. Still, even though I've given up any hope of ever finding a decent guy, it's still fun to look around and see what's out there. Just for old time's sake." The fact that her voice had risen three octaves was duly noted.

Cindy sucked in a fresh breath of oxygen.

The ingredients practically assembled themselves. Wheat flour, oats, sugar, eggs, oil, baking soda... Cindy tapped her foot. Oh, yeah, the recipe! She flipped open the tattered book to her last concoction—Queens Muffins, which the kids had devoured last week in unscrupulous haste. On the next page sat a close-up picture of molasses-raisin muffins. Oh boy!

A heart-stopping moment. Did she have molasses?

"Are you even listening?"

Yes! Molasses to the rescue, right next to the Karo syrup. Cindy eyed the half-full black bottle with a practiced eye. It would do. A little brown sugar could make up for any deficiencies. She rolled up her sleeves and dove into baking mode.

"News around town is that John and Megan have split. You know anything about that?"

Cindy's eye twitched. Three friends had politely informed her of the shocking news. How shocking could it be in a world with a divorce rate running faster than the national debt clock? She tossed a prayer to Heaven. *God, help John and Megan. Even more importantly—help their kids.*

She preheated the oven, sprayed the muffin tins with olive oil, and poured her friend a glass of iced tea. "You sneer at every man you meet, tell your mom that you're entering a convent at the next summer solstice, and cater to your kids like they own the keys to the Kingdom of Heaven."

Jan actually frowned. Umbrage incarnate. "Do you have a point you're trying to make?"

After a you-know-darn-right-well wave, Cindy scooped up gooey spoon-fulls and filled two muffin tins. "Dear-heart, you have a nasty habit of dipping into poisoned wells, and then you wonder why you feel sick." She popped the trays into the oven.

Time to clean up.

Violins ready? Jan clasped her hands in pitiful desperation. "I just can't give up on love."

Cindy wondered if Elon Musk would allow her on board a spaceship heading—anywhere. "For Heaven's sake. Give love a chance—by all means. But love is a universe apart from happiness and romance." She wiped her hands on a dishrag. Vigorously. "Love is scrubbing the bathtub and getting off the grimy rings, making fried egg sandwiches for kids who seriously believe that they're starving when they have no clue, filling in paperwork with black ink and writing legibly, doing your civic duty even when it means you can't bring electronics into the courthouse, stopping at red lights, and not racing around tractors on a hill." Cindy tossed a drying towel to her friend.

Jan caught it handily.

Patrick jogged into the room. He jogged everywhere. If he wasn't jogging, he was eating or asleep. "Hey, Mom, I'm starving." A statement of fact. Nothing more.

A frantic screech. Kelly skedaddled into the kitchen, arms circling, ready for takeoff. "Fred's gone!"

Starvation would have to wait. Duty called. With an authoritative slouch, Patrick nudged his sister in the arm. "Naw. I just put him in his ball to roll around the house, so he won't spend the whole night on that rickety wheel."

Jan snorted. "With so much exercise, that rodent will outlive us all."

Kelly sniffed. "What's cooking?"

Cindy took a sip of tea and wondered which Fred liked better—the wheel or the ball.

Funny How Life Goes

Originally published on The Writings of A. K. Frailey
6/5/2020

Who knew that staring at the neighbor's backyard, watching for signs of life, could be considered nosey?

I wondered if the whole concept of "Mind your own business" was carried just a tad too far. After all, I hadn't seen hide or hair of the old man for weeks. He could've been dead for all I knew.

Or worse.

He could've turned into something… Okay, that image stemmed from last night's horror flick that my teen son had insisted wasn't scary. It all depends on if *scary* meant I freaked out on the couch or simply spent the entire day picturing my eighty-something neighbor as an alien experiment.

"Can I help you?"

Oh, great. The son. He caught me red-handed…actually wide-eyed. I turned from the fence, amazed that he had snuck up so close. Gravel roads usually gave people away. And where were my lousy dogs? I gazed around. Sure enough. Napping in the sun…probably didn't even lift their heads as this veritable stranger strolled up the driveway.

I faced the fifty-something gentleman and smiled brightly, frantically thinking up a good lie. Unfortunately, my mouth tends to leave the station before my brain is finished giving instructions.

"I just wanted to see if Mr. Jacob is still alive."

A low whistle.

Well, I hit the prize impression with that one. "I mean…I haven't seen him for a while, and he's been on my mind."

"He's fine." The man's eyes stared at me as if an interrogation room was being contemplated. Dang, but he'd have the whole alien experiment thing outta me before I could get properly tied to the chair.

So, what now? The guy is standing between me and my back door. I could skirt around him, pretending that I'm just ambling toward my garden to pick— Heck, it's full of seedlings too young to touch, and with my daughter's ruthless war on weeds, there wasn't even a stupid dandelion to hide behind.

He clasped his hands and continued to stare as if he wanted to talk. Probably not about aliens.

The only decent thing to do was stand there and take it. Yes. I've been nosey. I'd imagined gosh-awful possibilities all day until I just had to sneak over and see if poor Mr. Jacob could still walk…or crawl…around his place. And no, I wouldn't appreciate it if someone else was watching me with an overloaded imagination ignited by horror movie scenes.

Thoroughly ashamed was I.

He cleared his throat. Always a good sign. It meant he'd like to tell me off but was holding himself back.

"Dad's been off his feed for weeks. My sister is spent taking care of her daughter who broke her leg and has three little ones to corral. I've got to go out of town for the weekend, and I was just wondering if you'd keep an eye on him for a couple of days."

My brain couldn't back up fast enough. For a moment, I actually believed I had lost the power of speech. Which is darn unusual for me. "Uh...well...sure...I'd...be happy...to."

"Pa thinks he can manage everything himself. But you know, he watched some scary movie last night and thought you were coming to get him for some kind of alien abduction thing." The guy actually laughed.

At me!

I could've wept in relief.

"Oh, how silly!" I grinned good-naturedly. After all, I am a decent human being. From planet Earth no less. Heck, I now imagined baking this man the nicest pie in creation—after I fed his dad a delicious non-alien dinner.

Funny how life goes. When I stopped by that first evening, Mr. Jacob backed up against the wall, apparently expecting my pie cutter to slice through more than crust, but when I unveiled the cherry pie, all was well.

Now I go to the fence nearly every day and stare until Mr. Jacob or his son comes out to chat. Occasionally I call ahead. But usually, they seem to just feel my presence. We meet up and talk. I might bring a pie. The son might bring a couple of beers. Mr. Jacob brings his smile.

And so far...no aliens.

Rest Awhile

Originally published on The Writings of A. K. Frailey
5/22/2020

Deb loved the universe—and Beyond. It was mutual.

But the facts remained. Her friends and relations contradicted nearly everything she said, and her husband grinned wickedly whenever she used the words, "I've been thinking…"

Yet the oaks and maples swayed in exuberant joy whenever she strolled near the tree line bordering their property. Almost as if they spoke through motion, "Welcome, friend. Lay down your burdens. Rest awhile."

If only—

A small body barreled into her. Jody, her youngest, was master of the yard and could roam from the front lawn to the back barbecue with complete freedom. Still, once she stepped off the porch, he inevitably pelted her direction and threw his arms around her legs as if he had not seen her for—what? How do six-year-olds measure time? Hours? Days? Clearly not years since he believed that she was older than the moon.

"Mom?"

"Yes, dear?"

"Can you play with me?"

Her shoulders sagged. Jody's plea weighed on her shoulders like a boulder carried over a turbulent stream. The clicking-clacking sound of the drier rolled in the background. *Must've left*

Clifton's belt on his pants... She winced at the image of metal scraping metal.

"Deb?"

Her husband stood on the porch.

Deb shaded her eyes from the bright May sun. "Yes, honey?"

"You seen my belt?"

A number of lies jumped to the tip of her tongue. Would evasive half-truths work? "Uh..."

"It's in the drier!" Jody beamed, proud of the "eagle eye" Daddy assured him he was born with. "Mom threw it in there."

Caught like a rat in a trap.

"Hon-eeey!" That last drawn-out syllable said it all.

In desperation, Deb glanced at the trees. The maple branches swayed wildly though the wind wasn't strong. Their offer of friendship stretched across the yard in a valiant attempt to calm her turbulent stomach.

She patted her son's head. "I can't play now; we've got company coming for dinner. But Uncle Ben is always up for a game of catch."

Jody's eyes widened. Uncle Ben—like superman—flew in, amazed anyone under the age of seven, and then flew away like a superhero ready to accomplish his next mission.

The gleeful little boy shouted and frightened a robin from her nest. She fluttered to a higher branch while the boy dodged around his dad, intent on serious matters. Perhaps he'd clean his room? Fling his books and toys on the floor looking for a treasure to show his uncle more like.

Clifton plunked down the steps. His irritation over the belt forgotten in light of this newest doom. "Ben? *Tonight?*"

The branches slowed, subdued by the grim news. Another robin fluttered near and chirped a brave song of defiance.

There was never a good night for Ben, according to Clifton. Opposites on politics, religion, and how to properly open a can of beer, they saw eye-to-eye on absolutely nothing. Except mutual distrust bordering on hate. On that, they might actually agree.

"He asked if he could come by… What could I say? He wants to see Jody."

Clifton gave her *THE LOOK*—head down, eyebrows up, eyes searing her brain like laser beams. "It took the man three years to realize that his nephew's name isn't Joel."

The maple limbs drooped. A few baby leaves quivered. The joy of living barely vibrated in the still air.

"He wants to care." Weariness enveloped Deb. The drier stopped with a long screech like a train arriving at the station. She could retrieve the clothes, return the missing belt, and lift one guilty burden off her shoulders. Jody would play with Ben and—whoosh—another guilt-rock would roll away. For a few minutes.

Her husband snorted.

Her spirits smashed to earth. She stared at the ground. Or was it quicksand?

"Well, if he's coming, I'm going. I've got some work I can do at Dad's."

Deb nodded. It was the most reasonable solution. “You want me to send some of the fried chicken over? You two could make a—”

“Naw. I’ll get pizza. We’ll be fine. He’ll scream at the politicians on TV and then fall asleep after a couple of bites.” He shrugged. “You know how he is. Never happy. But at least I can fix the bathroom sink in peace and quiet.”

Torn, Deb knew that Clifton would mutter under his breath when he couldn’t find some tool or another, but he’d get the job done. He always did.

The phone buzzed in her pocket. She grabbed it. Lia? Deb tensed, ready for anything between a molehill and an atomic explosion.

Clifton frowned.

She showed him the name and then plastered the phone to her ear. “Hey, Lia!” Her tone sounded much too cheerful.

Three states away, Lia could still moan like a cow mooing directly in your ear. “I’m soooo siiiick! Mom’s taking me to the doctor.” Sniff. Cough-cough. “I just want you to know that if she crashes us or something, it isn’t my fault.”

After living a thirty-year soap opera, Deb knew her lines perfectly. She used the right pitch, oohhed and awed appropriately, and hit the end button as soon as decently possible.

She looked up. The real world still existed. Except, now her husband was stomping away from the fence bordering the Chelsea Estate. Or such was the name etched into an enormous boulder at the base of their neighbor’s fifteen-foot driveway.

“Something wrong?”

“That witch says Jody plays too loud in the morning and wants us to keep him inside till ten so she can get her beauty sleep.”

Deb winced. “Well, he does get rather loud—inside or out. I’ll have a talk with him and find something quiet he can do till mid-morning.”

“No wonder she’s always running to a therapist after every breakup. No sane human would put up with her.”

“She’s had a hard life.”

Clifton slapped his hand against his cheek, his eyes alarmingly wide. “Of her own making.”

There was no point in denying the obvious. “I’ll get your belt.” Deb sighed and clasped the porch railing.

Rolling his shoulders, Clifton clearly wanted to start the day over. He stepped in front of her. “It’s okay. I’ll get it.” His face flushed pink. “I spilled some taco sauce on it the other day—it needed a wash.” He patted her arm, a quick massage with his thumb. A smile twitched, his eyes laughing. “I don’t know how you do it.”

A gust of wind sent delicious shivers over her skin, and the rustle of leaves tickled her ears. “What?”

“Put up with us.” Her husband chuckled. “Your brother’s an idiot, and my dad’s a tyrant.” He climbed the porch steps. “Your sister’s crazy, the neighbor has a screw loose, and the world is going to hell.” He stopped in the doorway and grinned back at her. “Yet, you never seem to care.”

Deb watched her husband saunter into the house. He whistled a happy tune. All his irritations blown away like dust on the wind.

The tree limbs begged with frantic waves for her to come and visit.

She strolled over. Reaching up, she stroked the smooth bark and soft leaves. The rustling leaves danced in frantic joy.

Her spirit responded in kind.

Lifting her face to the sun, she closed her eyes and abandoned herself. Every sense in her body—and Beyond—filled with peace. “I do care.”

I Don't Have to See Christmas

Originally published on The Writings of A. K. Frailey
5/8/2020

"Ya know...you'll never live to see the nuts ripen from that tree. Much less eat them."

George grunted as he pressed the shovel deeper into the sod. He didn't look up, but his grunt served a dual purpose. At eighty-three, it took every ounce of his strength to dig even a moderately deep hole. This one had to be large enough to bed a well-rooted sapling. The woody mate stood proudly to the side, evidence that George's tenacity hadn't dwindled with the years. He glanced aside. Had his guttural response made his point quite clear?

Randy sucked a hard candy and nodded. "You know what I mean, though."

Stabbing the earth to create a soft landing, George turned the shovel in every direction he could and broke up the larger clumps. Satisfied, he motioned to the arboreal infant.

Obliging, Randy placed the root ball in the center of the hole. Together the two men shoved loose earth around the exposed plant. Randy lugged a twenty-pound bag of luxurious soil to the edge and using both hands, poured the rich blackness around the trunk, creating an even mound.

"That'll do." George sloshed a five-gallon bucket of water to the edge and tipped it near the base. The mound melted like sugar in tea.

Randy poured more dirt and sucked the last of his candy bits from his teeth. "You're doing this for grandkids, then?"

A woman's voice called from the doorway. "Dinner's ready. You boys better hurry up or it'll get cold. Janie's going to stop by on her way to the bank and pick up that piece you want repaired. Better be washed up."

Randy shook his head as he tossed the nearly empty dirt sack over his shoulder. "What's the bank got to do with a well pump, I want to know. That woman just likes to run around town. All day and every day."

The empty bucket banged against George's knee as he walked. "The grass is always greener..."

As they entered the kitchen door, the smell of fried chicken, baked potatoes, boiled asparagus, and brownies smacked into them like the first day of summer vacation. Olfactory nerves did a happy dance.

Selma looked Randy up and down, apparently considering whether to send him back out the door or let him stay. "You get that last quarter done?"

"Sure. I just stopped by to see if—uh..."

Selma patted the tall man's arm. "Well, you can eat and then help Janie put that pump part in her car." She glanced at the laden table, ticking items off her fingers. "Oh, shoot, the butter!" She twirled and shot off, a heat-seeking missile after a new target.

Randy slipped into the nearest chair, silent as a mouse sniffing the cat's dinner dish.

A woman wearing a composition of pink jeans, a sky-blue blouse with matching sandals, and jingling earrings, bounded into the room, pulled up short, and pressed her hand against her chest. “Thank God! I was afraid I’d find you all laid out on the floor.”

Sliding the butter dish beside a tall stack of bread, Selma eyed her cosmopolitan daughter. “We don’t usually eat on the floor, darling. Why’d we start now?”

George came in drying his hands on a towel. He worked his way around his DNA replica and dropped the towel in Randy’s lap.

Randy took the hint, slid out of the chair, and headed for the tiny washroom off the kitchen door.

George plunked down at the head of the table and answered his wife’s question. “She heard that the economy is collapsing, our leaders are fools, there are twenty-three new ways to die, and—rumor has it—a comet is heading directly for earth.”

Randy poked his head out the washroom doorway, a confused frown running riot over his forehead. “Does that mean that the sky is falling—literally?”

With admonishing fingers, Selma waved the obscene consideration into oblivion. “This fried chicken won’t get any tastier just sitting here.”

“But, mom!” Janie’s hoops danced. “We have some really big problems to discuss—”

George clasped his hands and bowed his head. “They’ll wait till after dinner.”

Prayers said.

The meal commenced.

Selma was right.

The dinner could not have been tastier.

As he scooted his chair back, George peered from his wife to his daughter and finally landed on his nephew. "You asked if the nut trees are for the grandkids." His gaze bounced off his daughter. "If we ever have any."

Randy wiped his mouth, his eyes rolling upward, a clear attempt to retrieve his languid thoughts from the morning. "Yeah. Well...it'll take a long time for those trees to mature, you know."

Selma stopped; plates piled high on her left arm, her right swinging a dishcloth. "You planted them!" Her gaze softened, and she scurried to the window. Craning her neck, she smiled, unloaded the dishes, returned to her husband, and threw her arms around his neck. "You are the dearest man alive!"

Janie shook her head. "Like nut trees are going to do any good. We'll be lucky to see next Christmas the way things are going!"

In an act of open defiance, Randy tipped back his chair—normally a no-no. "To be honest...I don't see the point, either. Janie's divorced and neither of us has kids...so who—"

"I don't have to see Christmas to believe that someday, someone will enjoy those pecans."

Selma wiped her sentimental, tear-filled eyes. "I told George I wanted him to show me that he loves me—in a new way."

"What do pecans—?"

George chuckled. "She always loved those nuts. So, when I proposed, I put a ring on the top of a pecan pie and gave it to her."

Randy's chair legs hit the ground, his eyes wide, taking in unrealized vistas of reality. "I never knew you had it in you—"

Janie straightened her shoulders and shot to her feet. "We're just wasting time. I'd better get that pump part. At least I can do something useful."

Randy took his cue, stood and bowed his gratitude to Selma. He pressed George's shoulder as he followed his cousin out the door. "Never would've guessed."

Selma sighed, reaching for her husband's hand, her wedding ring glinting in the noonday sun as it poured through the kitchen window. "She doesn't understand, does she?"

George stood and wrapped his arms around his wife. "Few do."

It Takes Time

Originally published on The Writings of A. K. Frailey
4/24/2020

Marge wondered how it would feel to break her leg. Or arm. Or maybe just a finger. A toe? Would a hangnail suffice? Perhaps a bad headache. Some quality reason for staying in bed way past her usual wake-up call.

She opened her eyes.

Oh yeah. Real-life. The world. Trial. Tribulation. Mistakes and Mayhem.

Sleep?

She dragged herself to the bathroom—washed her face and wondered if a bang on the head would induce amnesia. There was so much to forget.

"Hey, Mom?"

"Yep."

"The coffee is ready, and there are rumors of breakfast."

Saturday? Good glory. She sniffed. Sausage and eggs. Coffee. After wrestling out of her pajamas and into her day clothes, she snatched a look out the window. Blossoms filled the hedgerow. The apple trees were on a roll. Even the maples joined the fun, sending seedpods whirling through the air.

She sauntered into the warm kitchen while Jon and Kelly perched on stools at the counter, plates set. Food ready. Their fingers wrapped around coffee mugs from which swirls of hot steam unfolded like vaporous petals.

A glance at the crucifix. A breath of prayer. *Lord, forgive us. We don't know what we're doing.*

Kelly sloshed orange juice into her tall glass and took a sip. She smiled. "I wondered if you were ever going to get up."

Jon shot his sister a warning glance.

Marge gratefully poured rich black coffee into her special mug. A birthday gift. Last year. An eon ago, it seemed. She leaned against the counter. "I just decided to take my time. Luxuriate in the reality of having nothing important to do."

Jon shook his head.

Meg's face imitated one of those Salvador Dali paintings, drooping like melting waxworks.

"You still have us." Jon's words barely broke the tension in the room.

She wanted to say—*And you still have me.* But for how long would that be true?

Her stomach clenched in tight knots, and there was little hope of actually enjoying breakfast. But it would be cruel to refuse their offerings. Their kindness in making a good breakfast. She pulled her plate forward and sized up the fried egg, sausage, and toast as if they were enemies to conquer rather than food to digest. Like a warrior, she nodded and set to battle.

With a great deal less drama, her children did much the same.

~~~

Once out in the garden, Marge found herself relaxing in the warm sun. The weeds had been kept in check, so there wasn't much to do. But
~~~

the border needed to be pulled back, especially around the potato hills. The cucumber vines had to be directed away from the tomatoes, or they'd break their fragile stems.

The padding of feet and huffing of breath made her sit on her haunches. She reached over to give Old Sheba a quick pat. She brushed against a pant leg and almost fell back in surprise.

A tall, lean, brown-haired boy stood aside, staring down at her. Sheba was indeed there, sitting next to him as if this stranger were a guest she planned to introduce. The boy didn't say anything. Apparently, she was supposed to go first.

Marge stood and wiped her hands on her dusty jeans. "Hi, there."

"Hi." He glanced over his shoulder. "Mom said I could stop and see your garden. Ask you a question."

Marge wasn't surprised. She had learned long ago that everyone in these parts knew everyone else. She was an outsider. The ignorant one who'd be forever baffled by second cousins' great-grandma, brother-in-law's nephew, and various blended families with stepchildren.

"A question?" She wiped imaginary sweat from her forehead. "You can ask. Don't know if I'll have the answer, though."

He adjusted his glasses with the back of his hand and waved at the garden spread. "How'd you learn to do all this?" He shrugged. "Mom said that gardening skill is something you're born with. She wasn't lucky that way."

After the fact, Marge realized just how rude her snort must've sounded. People loved to say, "It just comes naturally." Ha! No siree-bob. Nothing natural about it. The boy was tall but too skinny. Poor thing. What was Unlucky Mom feeding this kid? White bread and canned beans?

"Look." She held out her hands. Thick fingers, broken nails, a few calluses, and enough wrinkles to send any lotion company into fits, advertised her imperfections. "These are the hands I was born with—but they never touched the dirt till I was a grown woman. I couldn't keep a house plant alive."

The boy—Slender, she'd call him—patted the dog at his side, not so much to comfort the animal, probably hoping to find a little support.

"But—" He glanced around at the glorious green bean vines, perfect little corn shoots, blossoming potato hills, budding zucchini plants, the whole luxurious garden breaking through the earth and soaking in the sun.

Marge shrugged. "In truth, my kids do most of the work."

"How'd they learn?"

"I taught 'em what mistakes I made so they wouldn't make the same ones. They studied books. Tried a new crop each year. Failed some. Succeeded some. Got better over time."

The slender child blinked, tilting his head as he stared at her. "But we need a garden this year."

Marge knew that. It weighed on her mind. Like so many things. "Who's your mom, honey?"

"Grandma Gale's youngest, Rosie. Holloway. My dad lives the next state over. Mom's staying with Grandma now. They've got the land, just not much energy. She thought maybe you could teach me. And I could...” He looked away. Dispirited.

The image of her daughter’s melting smile squeezed her heart till it broke into uncountable pieces.

Shame flooded Marge’s whole body. How could she be so selfish? It pounded over her like a torrent. Her sluggish attitude. Dragging herself to the fine breakfast her kids set before her. And her gifts. The ones she could offer. If she tried.

She pressed her hands to her chest. No hope of putting the pieces back together; she’d just have to let them melt in one fiery furnace and forge something new. Perhaps something stronger than a human heart.

She couldn’t promise to live tomorrow. She couldn’t fix all the problems that faced her...or the world...or her neighbors. But she had to admit; she did have one or two answers.

“Well, I’m not the gardening expert of the family. Jon is. Kelly raises the meat birds—if you care to see.” She pointed to the chicken coop fenced in with wobbly green netting rescued from an abandoned farm up the road. “They’re mighty tasty on a warm summer evening or during a fierce winter storm.”

He grinned up at her. “Can’t *you* do anything?”

Now her best snort bellowed. “Well, of course, I can! Why I make the best bread this side of the moon, child.”

He squinted. Testing her. Could she prove that?

In answer to the unspoken challenge, she dropped a hand on the boy's shoulder. "You just come inside, and I'll give you a piece. With butter. Maybe I have a loaf I can let your mom try. If she'd be interested, I can send her the recipe."

"She's not very handy in the kitchen."

"None of us are when we're born. It takes time. To learn. Anything."

"You think your son Jon might teach me about gardening?"

"Can't imagine why not. He's a reasonable fellow."

"And I could learn about the meat birds, too?"

"If you'd like." She nudged him along toward the house. "Come on in a moment. I'll get you that piece of bread and scrounge up a son or daughter—and we'll see what we can do."

The boy trotted at her side, one hand patting the dog in joyful abandon. Old Sheba jumped about like a pup ready for the first romp she'd had in years. He stopped a moment, his face sobering. "Mom said I shouldn't wear you out."

"Son, I only wished you'd been there to roust me out of bed this morning."

"You slept in late?"

"Almost slept my life away." She pointed her face toward the kitchen. "Now, where'd I put that recipe book?"

You Decide

Originally published on The Writings of A. K. Frailey
4/10/2020

Clyde was sure he was dead. Who survived a storm of this magnitude? In a car...sitting in the middle of a highway... He closed his eyes. If he was going to be blown to kingdom come, he didn't want to see it happen.

"Why'd we stop?" Dan, Clyde's neighbor and sometimes home-improvement partner, roused himself from sleep, rubbing his eyes and stretching like a kid after a long nap.

Clyde pointed ahead. "There's a barricade...some road problem, and it looks like the storm of the century is heading this way. Someone is trying to get people to turn around.

Dan rolled down the window and craned his neck out, swiveling right and left.

A long line of cars snaked ahead and behind into the dense gloom.

"We're not going anywhere in a hurry."

Clyde felt his heart drop to his boots. "If only."

Dan unstrapped his shoulder harness and pulled the door lever.

Clyde's heart did a one-eighty and jumped to his throat. "Hey, where the H are you going?"

Dan waved ahead. "Look, it's just a young guy. Some patrol officer is trying to steer everyone back." He chuckled. "It's like Fred Rogers facing down a pack of irritated hyenas."

"Yeah. Well, it's what he's paid to do."

A frown creased Dan's forehead. He leaned in and clamped his gaze on Clyde. "So you'd rather sit here and wait for the storm to toss us into never-never land?"

A baby squalled in the distance. Clyde dearly sympathized.

"Besides, you know Jennie would be irate as a pancake flipper with no spatula if you got killed in a spring storm. She has you pegged for a long-liver or a go-out-in-a-blaze-of-glory kind of guy."

Clyde felt a hot flush work over his face. "Ayah. I guess." He really would hate to disappoint his wife. Though she'd get along without him all right. The kids were all grown. The house was pretty much paid for, and there was a good life insurance policy, but she'd reeeeally hate to be left with— "He got carried away." —in his obituary.

The two strolled down the road, passing twenty-three cars. Clyde kept his face forward, avoiding eye contact. Dan, on the other hand, waved and grinned, apparently practicing for the role of the neighborhood ice cream man. *He ought to have a little bell.*

It was all too clear that sweat-stained the officer's armpits as he repeatedly lifted his arms in a futile effort to direct irate drivers to maneuver their vehicles to the side so some kind of turning zone could be arranged.

Clyde measured the growing storm with his eyes. He wondered if a sincere Act of Contrition would work for his Confession or if he was stuck with the full weight of the last three months I-don't-have-time-to-count-'em-now-sins.

Dan chewed his lip, swiveled his head forward and back, and then clapped his hands. He jumped up on the hood of the patrol car, waved, and shouted.

Clyde wanted to grab the officer's arm for support. Considering the look on the young man's face, the feeling must've been mutual.

"Hey! Hi, ya'll!"

Dizziness ensued. *Eyes can't really roll around like on those cartoon characters—can they?* Clyde peered askance at the officer. *Darn. Guess they can.*

The officer tried to recover command of the situation. "Excuse me. I'm—"

Dan smiled down. A benevolent benediction if ever there was one. "Yes, sir! You're right, Officer. If everyone would steer their cars to the far right side, onto the shoulder here, (Lots of hand motions for those without brains.) there'd be enough for a turn lane."

Dan jumped down, directed the lead car to follow his example, and quickly assisted the driver to face the car in the right direction. The officer, his eyes steadied, his confidence returned, worked alongside. Together they maneuvered down the line, beckoning with rotating hand motions, calling, cajoling, and even teasing until, in a matter of moments, a flow of traffic started away from the impending storm.

Once salvation was at hand, the masses knew what to do. And they did it. As fast as their wheels could carry them.

The patrol officer waved with a grateful grin as Clyde maneuvered his car away. The storm still appeared menacing, but there was a decent chance they'd make it home before it struck.

Another patrol car zipped by on its way to assist the lone officer. Clyde shook his head. “There’s a reason I’m not a cop.”

Dan nudged him. “Or a doctor.” He closed his eyes and leaned back.

A flush reheated Clyde’s face. “What’s that supposed to mean?”

Dan opened one eye.

Clyde slowed for the turnoff. Only five miles to go. Raindrops sprinkled the windshield. He smacked the wiper switch and grunted his disapproval of raindrops and cryptic comments.

Dan sat up. He glanced out the window as slashing drops obscured the fields and woods. “You’re not a leader, Clyde. You don’t want to be. You’re happy for someone else to step up.”

“That’s not true!” Clyde’s face burned with righteous indignation. “I wrote to the county commissioner about our sewer problem. I stood up at the school board meeting and told off principal what’s-his-face that one time. I even re-tweeted—”

Dan lifted his hand. “I didn’t say that you haven’t complained.”

Furious drops pelted the windshield. Clyde’s grip tightened, and his jaw clenched. He slowed the car to a crawl as his heart pounded in tune with the storm.

Lights glimmered in the distance; the faint outline of a farmhouse shimmered through the rain-drenched window. Dan’s wife, Gloria, would be worried, but she’d pretend she wasn’t. She’d laugh off her fears and welcome her husband from the front porch with beckoning arms. He’d sweep her into a bear hug, swing her around, and they'd go inside to dance or make love.

Clyde halted the car, undoubtedly splashing mud up the side in the process. “You want to explain that?”

Dan shook his head. “Not really. But honestly, Clyde. Come on. You live inside a fear-filled box. You bang on it by complaining. But when something needs doing, you wait for someone else to step in.”

“So, I'm not a big know-it-all.”

“Look, buddy. I'm not trying to be cruel. But, truth is…well.”

Stomach-churning anger swirled inside Clyde. “Damn it. I never expected this from you, Dan. I thought you had my back. I thought—” In a rush of fury, he jabbed a shaking finger at the passenger door. “Just get out. You can walk the rest of the way home. I've got to get back to Jennie. At least she really cares about me.”

Dan placed his hand on the door lever and stopped. “I had your back…and your front…today. I always do. But soon that won't be true. I've got cancer, man. Chances are… But that doesn't matter. Fact is; death comes for us all.” He swung his head like an exhausted bull and stared at Clyde through weary eyes. “You got to decide if you're going to keep complaining and following…or if you're going to start solving.” He shrugged. “It's up to you.”

Clyde stared as the wavering form of his friend climbed the steep porch steps. He wasn't sure, but he thought he could see Gloria's shape as she stepped down to meet him. Yep. They embraced.

Slowly Clyde maneuvered the car around and started toward home. One mile up the road. The rain lightened, but his vision remained blurred.

This time, he'd keep his heart as well as his eyes open.

We're Not Neanderthals

Originally published on The Writings of A. K. Frailey
3/27/2020

Sydney knew he faced mission impossible, but he had to try. She'd never be a fully functioning human being until she joined the ranks of millions—no billions—who had gone before her and embraced the brave new world.

He felt the gravel crunch under his tires as he turned into the driveway. The back gate was closed, which meant that the goat was probably in the barn, safe and sound, thank God. He'd spent the entire weekend either catching up on house repairs, work reports, or alternating with his wife at one of the kid's weekend games. *What idiot scheduled soccer practice twice a week and games on Sunday?*

He took the key out of the ignition. Four o'clock. He might as well get this over with. Mom and Dad ate a formal dinner at noon and a light supper at six. Promptly. He hardly wanted to try squeezing the whole technological world in between the early news and grilled cheese & tuna sandwiches.

But try, he must. He grabbed the Kindle from the passenger seat and lumbered from the car, huffing with the exertion. Darn, but he should've had another cup of coffee before coming. He felt in his pockets. A handful of chocolate-covered coffee beans ought to do the trick.

Munching, he climbed the steps up to the porch and pressed open the door with a "Hey, anyone home?"

"Sydney!"

As if she didn't expect to see me. Hah! Sydney felt a rush of guilt. For what, he wasn't sure and wouldn't stop to think about it. *Roll away, guilt. Just roll away.*

"Hey, Mom." The hug. The warm kitchen. The sense that nothing ever changed. Though she was a bit older. Moved slower as she crossed the room. "Dad here?"

"Oh, he's out back with the dogs. Taking care of one of the Kerns' pups. It got injured, and he's nursing it back to health."

"Nice of him. Never could say no."

His mom shook her head, smiling the way she always did. "Why would he? He likes dogs. You know that." She peered at her son.

Sydney felt like he time-warped back to yesterday's airport security. What a horrible flight. The baby crying, the guy snoring, the storm clouds looming.

"You okay, son?"

Sydney shook himself. "Sure." He laid the Kindle on the counter. "I brought it like I said I would."

A combination of fear and distaste flickered over his mom's seventy-year-old face. "That was nice of you. But I don't really need it. I've got two library cards and that flip phone you gave me last year."

"But, Mom, this is so much easier. You won't have to get out in the weather to go to the library. Books come to you. Right here. In your hands." He lifted the Kindle like a car salesman showing off his latest option. He shrugged the image away.

With a long sigh, his mom picked up a long-handled spoon and stirred a pot bubbling on the stove. "I made chili—used up the last of the frozen tomatoes, onions, and peppers. I even tossed in a can of homemade salsa for zest. We've got enough hamburger to last into May, but dad says he's gonna butcher that old cow. She's never recovered since the fall she had, and he figures she'd be enough to give you and Heidi some and still last us until next year."

Sydney pictured the last package of hamburger he bought at the store—unnaturally red and outrageously priced. Had a strange taste too. "Well, I never say no to your food. The kids love your cooking more than me, I think."

"Oh, honey. Don't be silly. It's just that we spent so much time with them when they were little." A wistful expression spread over her eyes. "It's good that they're involved in so many activities now, but I hope they won't forget Grandma and Grandpa..."

As if he could stop a knife twisting his innards, Sydney clutched the Kindle harder. "Well, let's get down to business, shall we?"

A defeated damsel, his mom laid the spoon aside, pulled out a wooden kitchen chair and sat down. "You can show me, but I can't promise I'll remember..."

"Just try, Ma. It's all I ask. Do it for me. This way, I don't have to worry about you going out in all kinds of weather just to get to the library. Or doing so many things you don't have to do. There are more than books on here. You can get music and movies. You can look up—"

Like a zealot cajoling a wayward member of the flock back into the fold, Sydney showed off the cyber universe with finesse and confidence.

The back door slammed. Dad strode in, slightly bent but grinning from ear to ear. "Got that pup fed, its leg splintered, and now she's sprawled out with the hounds like she's never known any different."

Looking up like a drowning woman begging for a lifeline, his mom stared at her husband through a plastered smile. "Look what Sydney brought us."

Discomfort sent prickles over Sydney's spine. "Oh, Dad don't care about this stuff. He's told me so a hundred times."

With a snort, his dad splashed his hands under the tap, scrubbed vigorously with soap, then rinsed and dried like a professional hand washer. He sniffed the chili, hobbled to his chair, and plunked down with a happy sigh. "You make it sound like I hate what you do, son. I don't hate it."

"You've never taken any interest in it, that's for sure. Every time I try to show you what I do for a living, you turn away. Or say you don't understand. When I know you could—if you wanted to."

Dad and mom exchanged a quick glance, understanding each other in a way that strangled Sydney's heart.

Sydney closed the Kindle. Defeat weighed a couple of tons, at least. *Mission impossible. I knew it.*

Nudging him in the shoulder, his dad offered an encouraging smile. "You're not listening, son.

I appreciate what you do. Your technology skills amaze me. Your mom and I are very proud of you. We just have better things to do than join in on everything."

"Join in? What are you talking about? I'm just offering a Kindle device so she can get—"

Mom placed her hand over Sydney's and patted with maternal tenderness. "I *like* to go to the library. My friends are there. We chat and share what we're reading, tell about things going on in town, the latest news. Last week when I wanted a new way to fix venison, Jan found a great recipe online. She even identified that weird bug your dad found in the woodpile the other day from some etymologist in India."

She gazed into her memory. "Interesting man. Wish India weren't so darn far away." She glanced at her husband, and once again, they agreed in a silent conversation. "Your dad got his email address and is thinking of writing and asking how the bug managed to find its way into our backyard."

Sydney swallowed. "You've been on the web?"

Bernie grinned, leaning back against the sink, one brown, gnarled hand propped on the counter. "Of course. We're not Neanderthals. We just don't want to get all caught up in that stuff. It's fine now and again. But when Jill and the kids come over, they spend more time staring at their phones than talking with us. It's like they can't put the things down for even a minute." He shrugged. "Your mom and I have other things we like to do with our time." A twinkle entered his eyes as he met his wife's gaze.

A shocking, mischievous spark danced from husband to wife. Thankfully, Mom recovered quickly and swung her full attention to her son.

"You understand?" Mom's eyes pleaded.

Sydney heaved his body from the table. "So you don't want this?"

"It's just—we'd rather not be tempted." Dad clapped his hands together. "Now when are we going to have that chili? I'm as hungry as a bear after a long winter."

Mom hopped up and flipped open the cabinet. She grabbed bowls and charged into the utensil drawer, gunning for action, "Can you stay and have some, Sweetheart? I've got garlic bread warming in the oven."

Sydney pictured the scene at his home. His kids would each be in their room staring at their computers...or Kindles. Jill would be slouched on the couch—maybe playing a game or binge-watching her latest TV obsession. He'd walk in, say hi, but no one would respond. He'd go to his room and turn on his computer.

He peered down at the eager, alive faces of his parents and sat back down.

The Delete Button

Originally published on The Writings of A. K. Frailey
3/13/2020

"Modern technology is decimating my literary prowess as well as my love life."

Evangeline held her gaze steady, refusing to give in to an auto-eye-roll. *I love my cousin. Mom loves her. Dad loves her. I can't kill her without due process of the law.* She snatched a pecan from the trail mix bag and eyed it carefully.

"What? You think a nut can explain my life?"

There were so many possible responses—Eva's head swam. She popped the dainty morsel into her mouth and crunched. She peered over the top of her reading glasses at her DNA-sharer and wondered how any one human being could get so thoroughly confused on a daily basis. "What has the computer done to you now, Tracy?"

"The blinking delete button!"

Another pecan followed the first. Eva glanced at the car's dashboard. Six minutes to go. Once the kids were out of school and slumped into the back seat, they all could race to the store, pick up the cake mix and two kinds of frosting for the bake sale, plus three kinds of sprinkles because kids these days won't shell out their parent's money without sprinkles, speed home, get the girls on baking duty, let the dog out...no, definitely let the dog out first. Then preheat the oven. Then get the girls baking...

"Don't you want to know about the delete button?"

Eva propped her head against the warm car window. Four minutes. She could live through four more minutes, surely. "So what evil has the delete button been perpetrating upon you, my dear?"

"I don't have one when I talk."

Eva groaned.

"You know, I've won awards for my writing. I'm considered one of the most professional science journalists out there. But heck, put a mike in front of my mouth or perch a good-looking guy on the stand, and I'm a babbling idiot."

A tiny piece of pecan had wedged itself behind one of Eva's front teeth and it was worth more than the cost of her new couch to get the thing into a more approachable position. She took a sip of water as the school bell buzzed.

Kids swarmed like bees in springtime. The two second cousins, Kala and Marci bustled along bumping shoulders, as if they had just shared a joke or were in on a secret together.

At least, they looked like they were having fun. Eva pressed the unlock button. The kids tumbled in. End of conversation. She hoped.

Tracy dashed such dreams to smithereens without conscious thought. "My theory is that human beings are going to kill each other before the century is out because we're used to editing our words with the ease of a delete button, and we're slowly but surely losing the ability to speak coherently face to face." She turned and squinted at the girls with a two-fingered wave. "Hi, beautiful babes."

Eva didn't have to look in the rearview mirror to see the eye-rolls. The car nearly lurched into oncoming traffic with the force of them.

Marci patted her mom's shoulder. "Hi, pretty mama." She nudged Kala. They both grinned.

Eva made a slow turn into the store parking lot, which happened to be conveniently located between the grade school and the high school.

"Some city planners in cahoots with local business interests."

"What?" Tracy's wide-eyed expression left no doubt that the delete button was missing in action again.

Eva shook her head and darted from the stopped car like a puppy off its leash. "Sit tight. I just have to grab a couple things—"

No such luck. Tracy flew to her side and flung her purse strap over her shoulder. Soldiers had been known to carry injured buddies off the battlefield with less drama.

Speeding down the baking aisle, entertaining fantasies of finding both frosting and sprinkles on a half-off sale kept Eva's mind so busy she didn't hear a word her cousin said. Not until the babbling stopped short, and the woman's steely grip yanked her sleeve off her shoulder. "There he is! The guy I was interviewing today. He's a scientist. But you'd never guess, would you?"

With slow, nonchalant dignity, Eva redressed her shoulder and slid a glance at the scientist in aisle two. Indeed. He did not match any stereotypes currently running around Eva's married head. Except perhaps about some childish long-forgotten barbarian king with long, wavy hair, intense brooding eyes, broad shoulders and mighty biceps, who swept her off... Whoa—

Tracy strode forward and thrust out her hand.

Eva closed her eyes and thanked God that their innocent daughters were still in the car.

Tracy babbled. The man nodded.

Repeat.

Eva debated the need for Confession if she just slinked to the bakery aisle, retrieved her much-needed items, and then scraped her cousin off the floor after the fact. She turned, prepared for flight.

"Eva!" Tracy grabbed the man's hand and attempted the yank maneuver.

Eva froze, wondering if spontaneous combustion was a legitimate option.

By some kind of supernatural Grace, which apparently altered the known universe, the man grinned and allowed himself to be towed across two aisles.

Tracy beamed. Seriously. Beams of happiness shot from her eyes, nearly blinding Eva. "Guess what? I bet you'll never guess!"

Eva considered the guy. He appeared to be amused. Tickled even. His gorgeous physiology only accented his apparent joy.

Eva slapped her hand against her cheek.

The man laughed, pulled his hand free, and held it out. "I'm Kendrick and work at the state forensics lab. Your cousin interviewed me for—"

"He doesn't think I need a delete button!"

Eva shook her head. "But I do. Let the man finish his sentence."

Tracy blushed. "Oh, yeah. Sorry."

Kendrick's smile didn't waver. "It doesn't really matter. I was just glad we bumped into each other. I was rather short with her today, and I wanted to apologize. One of my kids has been sick, and I've been up two nights in a row helping my wife take care of him."

Without looking, Eva knew that Tracy's beam had faded into shadow. She offered the father a comforting shoulder pat. "Oh, been there, done that. Hope your boy gets better soon. Our girls are waiting for us in the car—we better run."

With a gentleman's nod, he returned to his niche aisle. Cold remedies and vitamins.

By the time they had returned to the car, Tracy had rediscovered her voice. "I didn't see a ring on his finger. So I just figured...and when he recognized me and said—"

Eva stopped beside the car and gave her cousin a one-armed hug, the other hand clutching the baking supplies. "Listen, honey, it isn't that you need a delete button—so much as a listening ear. Just give other people a chance to show you who they are before you decide you know them. Okay?"

Tracy nodded, yanked open the passenger side door and slid in with a harrumph.

Eva pulled into traffic, trying to decide if she should preheat the oven or hug her husband first.

You Never Know

Originally published on The Writings of A. K. Frailey
2/28/2020

As Lucy stared at the wafts of steam spiraling up from her cup into the frosty air, a bittersweet pang fluttered in her chest. *So like the incense they use at Mass.* Frankincense clouds rising toward the heavenly beings painted on the ceiling. She always felt like she was being left behind somehow.

She tapped her numb fingers on the mug to ensure circulation. It wasn't right, sitting here in the truck, out of the blasting wind, while the men dug the hole. Granted, they had a huge machine to do the digging. She only had to record the fact that the deed was done in the right place and mark it on the map. Perhaps she didn't need to be here at all.

But no. It was her job. Had been for years, and everyone trusted her to do it right. No one was ever buried in the wrong plot under her watch. A couple of families squabbled about who would go where, but that was quickly settled with cheerful tact and abundant patience.

But this time? There certainly were no squabbles. Even the deceased didn't specify exactly where he wanted to be buried. Only "in his hometown." He could have wanted to be buried in someone's basement for all she knew. Why didn't anyone ask him to clarify his wishes before it came to this? And put some money down while they were at it?

Lucy placed the cold mug in the cup holder and clapped her gloved hands together, sending prickling stings along her fingers. She could turn on the engine and warm up...but that'd be like telling the guys she was tired of waiting. Or too cold to stand it. They'd turn her way, looking apologetic. But then, they'd still have to get back to work and open the grave before it got any darker. Bothering them wouldn't make this go any faster.

With a sigh, her exhaled breath clouded the scene. She glanced at the folder in her lap. Might as well open it and appear to be doing her job. She flipped the thick, stapled papers to the last page. Section P. There were really only seven sections, A through F, and by all rights, this one ought to be labeled G, but someone around 1902 must've thought that future generations needed a little help keeping things straight. So, he or she labeled this section P. For pauper.

She didn't know much about Mr. Keelson. Oh, there were Keelsons living throughout the county. But this particular twig must've snapped off long ago since no one knew him or his history. When the funeral home called and said that a Mr. Thomas J. Keelson had left a scrawled note in the hospital, requesting to be buried in his hometown, she had recorded all the relevant info sure that, in time, some knowledge of him or his family would surface.

But no.

Mr. Thomas John Keelson was born in the town as the records stated, but not one person claimed him or his family. The Keelsons that lived over on Six Sisters Road had no idea who he belonged to. And Velma, the patriarch of the county, said she'd never clapped eyes on the man. It was a mystery. A sad one, at that.

A knock on the glass startled her. She looked up. Glen waved a couple stiff fingers with his dirty-gloved hand. His tight smile tried to appear cheerful, but his frosty white cheeks and squinting eyes bore testimony to a north wind that just wouldn't quit. He shouted through the glass as if the cold had made her hard of hearing. "We're ready."

She nodded and flipped the book back into her folder. She knew the lot number by heart. Seven-two-three. Block P. Three from the top. Three from the right. Nestled between Mrs. Eula Patel and open ground. There was an oak nearby, with an iron bench situated just under the heavy boughs. In the springtime, it looked picturesque. Today it sat between forgotten and forlorn. Her heart throbbed more painfully than the rheumatism in her joints. She climbed out of the truck and braced herself against the wind. She didn't even notice that she let her muttered thoughts loose as she tugged on her cream-colored crocheted mittens and then stuffed them into her oversized coat pockets.

"Why don't people think about the future? Surely..."

"What's that?" Glen, huffing through his scarf, still shouted. He tucked his hands under his armpits. His coat, as well as his frame, was so thin, she imagined that if the wind grew any stronger, it would surely knock him back all the way into block A.

"Oh, nothing. Just wondering why no provisions were made. It's not hard to pick out a plot, and they're not expen—"

"Family is probably all dead. Maybe he had one but gave it away like that Joseph guy in the bible did for Jesus."

Lucy shook her head and felt the wind bite her ears. She yanked her hood tighter around her head. Glen's gentle heart always looked for the best in folks.

Once she reached the graveside, she nodded to Paul. Short and stout to Glen's tall, lanky build, the two made a study of contrasts. Paul hardly ever said a word. Just did his work as carefully as ever a man could. A state inspector might review every grave dug in the last thirty years under Paul's watch but would never find a single fault.

The movement of the hearse backing up caught her attention. It stopped with the flash of the brake lights, and then the engine died. The door swung open and Berta swung out. The woman practically sprang from the front to the back like a released rubber band.

Being a funeral director, Berta had a certain gift for dramatic style. Despite the fact that there was no real assembly to speak of, the power of her movements retained their usual vigor. The back doors swung open, and the two men stepped forward in lockstep. The king's guard would've been impressed with the stately manner in which they carried the cheap wooden coffin from the hearse to the plot.

It took a bit of managing to get everything lined up just so, and the box down smoothly, but despite the wind howling in her ears, Lucy felt warm relief flood her whole body as Mr. Thomas J. Keelson was finally laid in his eternal resting place.

Once the process was completed to Berta's satisfaction, she grinned, waved, and then retreated from whence she had come like a motion picture star going off stage.

Glen and Paul began to fill in the hole. There was nothing left but to wait in the truck. Lucy climbed in, shoving her notebook and papers aside. It was too cold. She eyed the key in the ignition.

They won't mind.

The truck roared to life, and Lucy turned the heater on full blast. She leaned back in the seat and closed her eyes to the sound of the tractor shoveling dirt into the hole. She tried not to imagine it in her mind.

Her phone chimed.

After yanking off one mitten, Lucy tugged her phone from her coat pocket and smacked it against her ear. "Yes?"

"Mrs. Lucy Harden?"

"Speaking." Lucy felt her heart constrict. She didn't recognize the voice, but who on earth would be calling her this late on a Friday evening?

"Sorry to bother you, but I just discovered that my dad's body was taken to your cemetery to be buried."

"Your...*dad*?" A chunk of ice caught in her throat.

"Yeah. He'd been ill for some time and couldn't remember things so well. I've been living on the west coast. There's no one else. When he was sick, I made sure that the funeral home would do right by him...but I never actually specified where he was to be buried."

Lucy shook her head. Tears sprang into her eyes. "He left a note saying he wanted to be buried in his hometown. So we did." She grabbed a breath and choked it down. "Just now." Tears sprang into her eyes. "I'm so sorry. I didn't know you existed, or I would've let you know. The funeral home never told—"

"Oh, they didn't know. See, my dad and I didn't get along. He was a terrible dad, as a matter of fact, and a worse husband, if you know what I mean."

Lucy's gaze drifted to the two men adding the final touches to the grave, piling on the last of the dirt and rounding the edges. Their backs were bent and the oak's black branches seemed to claw the air above them like a menacing monster.

She made a proper grieving sound. As she must.

"But despite everything...I knew my dad was terrified of being cremated. He thought it was a prelude to hell. Used to say that if we had him cremated, he'd come back and haunt us. I figure he won't have any say in the matter...but still. I can't explain. I made sure he wasn't cremated. But I just couldn't bury him."

Lucy couldn't think of a thing to say. Her nose and ears burned like hellfire.

A knock on the window nearly wrenched her out of her skin.

"Done!"

Glen looked so happy through his dog-tired eyes, and Paul waved as he hustled to his own dirt-splattered truck.

Lucy nodded. To no one in particular.

Glen climbed in the driver's side, slapped his hands on the wheel, and grunted. "Thank God!" He saw her frown and froze.

Lucy spoke into the phone. "Sorry. But, what did you say your name was?"

"Oh, yeah. Thomas, like my dad. Though everyone just calls me Tom. Named my son Thomas too. Tommy. My wife insisted; she loves the name..."

A tear rolled down Lucy's cheek, and she couldn't for the world explain to Glen why she was crying. *I did my job, after all.*

"Well, Mr... I mean Tom. You can rest assured that your dad is buried properly. If you ever want to visit him, he's in section P."

"Thank you, ma'am. I just wanted to know. I doubt I'll ever come."

Lucy could hear Tom shift the phone against his ear.

"Maybe my boy will, someday. Never know."

Another tear followed the first.

"But I'm just glad it's over. Maybe now I can forget it all. Thanks...Bye."

Lucy stared at the silent phone as if it might dissolve in her hand.

Glen sniffed. "He had a son? Sorry he wasn't here to say a few words over his dad, I suppose. Poor guy. But he can come in the springtime—Memorial Day. We get a real crowd then. Maybe he'll even meet up with some long-lost family members." Glen put the truck into gear and headed onto the main road.

Lucy dropped her hands, still holding the dead phone, onto her lap. She stared at the houses with lit windows shining onto Main Street. Each a personality unto itself. Miniature little worlds.

Glen cleared his throat and jutted his jaw as if to defend a point of honor. "Well, you never know."

Lucy nodded. "You're right. You never know."

You Have No Idea

Originally published on The Writings of A. K. Frailey
2/14/2020

If electrical tape could talk, Shasta was sure the strip she held in her hand would scream, "I'm not made for this!"

Shasta batted away the hyper-personified thought and executed a swift fix. Only God and her electrician would ever know...and she wasn't talking to either of them at the moment.

A second razz from her doorbell told her that someone was getting a tad impatient. She eyed her work critically. Black electrical tape on a clear refrigerator shelf, cracked nearly in half, but oh well... She shoved the shelf back into its slot. *It works*. That had to be enough.

The bell sounded in two short bursts this time. "I'm coming!"

After running her fingers through her hair, Shasta smoothed down her rumpled sweater and figured that no one would notice that her shoes were broken down at the heel. Besides, the only people who came for a visit were salespeople who blatantly ignored the no soliciting sign posted on the edge of town or a couple of elderly religious ladies from a denomination Shasta kept getting mixed up with the local sports team: Vandals or Evangelical—something...

She swung open the door, prepared to be polite but firm. The answer was no.

"Hi, Shasta."

There he stood. Tall. Gray-headed. Heavyset. But still handsome. The train whistle in the distance could have carried the entire train with it, rumbled over her front lawn, heading directly for her, and she wouldn't have moved.

"Jasper?"

She blinked to make sure she wasn't hallucinating. Though she'd lived clean and sober all her life—one heard stories of strange events. *Carbon Monoxide poisoning?* She sniffed the air. *Nope.*

"Can I come in for a moment?"

Shasta backed up, opening the door wider, ignoring the cold wind rushing into the room. *Good Lord, he looks like mom.*

*It must've been twenty years...no...*she tried to calculate. She'd been living in Chicago the last time they'd talked. He'd been drunk and said some things he shouldn't have. She'd hung up on him...

"A long time, eh?"

Shasta dropped her gaze and considered dissolving into the floor. Her heart pounded, and spots swirled before her eyes. Jasper had gone from being a disturbed kid to a dysfunctional adult. When her mom got the police report that his body had been found in the park, she had grieved, but then relief had—

"I figure it was about twenty-six years ago we last spoke."

Thank God that good manners ruled society with habitual fluency. Shasta gestured to the couch. "Please, sit." She reached out. "I can take your coat."

He shrugged the heavy winter coat off his body and smiled as he handed it over. He wore an impeccable blue shirt with dark pants and gorgeous leather shoes.

Heaven, those shoes alone probably cost more than my monthly rent.

"Uh, you want some coffee…tea?" She only had cheap tea, but her coffee was pretty decent. *Something to make waking up in the morning worthwhile.*

"Only if you're having something."

Shoot. Shasta never had coffee in the afternoon since it would keep her up half the night, so she'd have to offer her bland tea. She eyed her brother again. He looked like he was used to having the best. *A drug dealer?* She shook her head and started for the kitchen.

"I'll just put the kettle on. My tea's not that great, but I can make it nice and hot—"

Jasper settled his large frame onto the couch. "Whatever you have is fine. Don't go out of your way."

Hmmm…this did not sound like the Jasper she knew. Her brother had always been wild and demanding. Flighty even. Nothing like this composed fifty-something gentleman making himself comfortable on her shabby sofa.

She slapped her cheek as she turned the fire under the kettle. She had patched a worn spot on the couch cushion with black thread, though the fabric was olive green because, well, heck, who has olive green thread?

She pulled two cups out of the cabinet, snatched a couple tea bags, dropped them into her finest mismatching mugs, and placed a jam-smeared creamer pot dead center. *Dang, I meant to wipe that—*

Jasper ambled into the kitchen, smiling.

Smiling? Certainly never like that. Shasta leaned on the counter. "Sorry, I'm a little befuddled. You've kind of taken me by surprise."

Jasper leaned on the sink and crossed his arms, his expression grave but not sad. Just serious. *A deep thinker? Jasper?*

"I thought about calling, but I was afraid you'd hang up on me."

Shasta had to give him credit. He didn't say "again" though the word hung heavy in the air.

Shasta shrugged. "I might have. I don't know. Usually, I try to give people a second chance—"

"Oh, but you did. And a third…a fourth…God knows how many. You and mom never seemed to give up. Always took me back in."

"But then you disappeared. We thought you were dead for a while there."

Jasper nodded. "That was kind of the point. I wanted to appear dead. Got mixed up with the wrong type of people…" He exhaled a long breath, his gaze on a trail she could not follow.

Shasta's body trembled. This was what was didn't want to live with…why she'd been so relieved—

"So, I died. Sort of. Actually, I did time in prison, gave testimony, met an amazing teacher, and started going to Mass again. Then I—" He met his sister's gaze. "I don't know how to explain it."

The kettle began to hum. "Like one of those reborn things people rave about?"

Jasper tilted his head. "That wouldn't do it justice. I got into a fight while serving my time and didn't win…if you know what I mean. I should've died. But for some reason, beyond everyone's hopes and expectations, I lived."

"Why didn't anyone tell me…or mom?"

"I wasn't going to drag you guys back into my mess. I never gave anyone your names. I wanted to either die or start over."

The kettle shrieked.

Shasta jumped.

Jasper laughed. "You always were sensitive."

Shasta poured the steaming water into the cups, a blush working up her cheeks.

Jasper stepped closer and leaned in. "I made you cry more than once, and I'm really sorry about that, Shasta."

Hot tears blurred Shasta's eyes. Hot water burned her fingers.

Jasper took the kettle and placed it back on the stovetop. He took both her hands and peered at her. "I was a terrible kid and a nasty man. I choose to tackle hell and take everyone who loved me through it too."

Her tears overflowed, and Shasta dropped her gaze. She wanted to wipe her face, but he still clutched her hands.

"I've made a new life, an honest one. Got married to a terrific lady and have three kids." He let go of her hands and pulled a wallet from his back pocket. He flipped the picture section open and four attached photos dangled in the air.

A pretty woman with stylishly cut hair and perky blue eyes stared at Shasta. A handsome teen boy dressed in a basketball uniform smiled, while a preteen girl and an adorable baby made up the rest of the family.

Something hideous stabbed Shasta from the inside. Sarcasm dripped like poison from a keen-edged knife. "Great, Jasper! I'm so happy for you.

When Mom died, I, like the dutiful daughter, managed everything. I even paid for her funeral and cleaned out the old house. The next year, my prince of a husband left me, saying that he'd rather travel the world than pay bills. So, I've been slaving away at a dead-end job for sixteen years, and now—" She squeezed her eyes shut, smacked her hands over her face, and bent double under a nameless agony. Uproarious sobs exploded like lava from an uncapped volcano.

Jasper bundled his sister into his arms and held her close, rocking her ever so gently.

She could hear his heart beating through his fine shirt. A spicy cologne scent wafted into her nose. Her shivering body responded to the sudden warmth.

His voice turned husky. Choking on the words. As if he were crying too. "That's why I've come back."

Shasta pulled away and stared at her brother. "Why? Because you feel guilty? Because you heard that my life isn't so great? That you've succeeded, and I'm a miserable failure?"

Jasper took his sister's hand and tugged her back to the couch. They sat side by side. He plopped his family photos on the coffee table, never noticing that she had used a brown marker to color in a water stain.

"Last Christmas, my two oldest kids—" he pointed to the appropriate photos as if she didn't have a brain in her head. "—got into an argument. Mary said some hard things to Dominic, and it got ugly fast. Everything was patched up after a bit...but the whole thing stirred some unpleasant memories."

Shasta swallowed and wiped the residue of tears off her cheeks.

"I told them that family is forever. But then, Mary pointed at me and asked where my family was. Dom waited, like he wanted to know too."

Shasta sighed. "Ouch, eh?"

Jasper threw back his head and stared at the ceiling. "I was convicted all over again. How could I tell my kids to forgive...to love each other through—whatever—when I had cut myself off from my own family?"

Shasta raked her fingers through her hair and straightened her shoulders. "You want to make amends?" She shook her head. "I never hated you or anything. It just hurt...that Mom died thinking the worst."

"I will live with that for the rest of my life. But you—" He swallowed and tears rolled down his face. "I don't deserve to be forgiven. I don't deserve another chance or the happy life I have. But...Shasta—I want to be able to tell my kids the truth. That family can forgive and love does—"

Shasta stood and waved to the kitchen. "Enough. I've cried enough for today. If you don't mind stale tea, I think I have a package of cookies in the fridge."

Jasper gave his face a quick rub down and followed Shasta into the kitchen. "What can I do to help?"

"Well, the cookies are in the crisper..." She put the teacups into the microwave and hit the minute button.

Jasper laid the package of Fig Newtons on the counter and smiled. "By the way, I like the black electrical tape on the shelf. Very chic."

Shasta grinned. "Oh, you have no idea, brother. You haven't seen anything yet."

Why Wait for Tomorrow?

Originally published on The Writings of A. K. Frailey
1/31/2020

Stella figured that—given the chance—she would definitely haunt her ex-husband. He needed a little something to make his life complete. And it might liven up her after-Earth experience. Sitting on a cloud all day must get rather dull.

Her daughter was trying on a new dress in the changing room. Something for a school dance next month. Not that Lindsey needed a new dress. She had plenty. But apparently, there was a new boy...

Stella sighed. The girl was only in high school. A senior. Okay. But still. She had her whole life in front of her. Why mess it up with a relationship she couldn't possibly handle? It would only bring heartache in the end.

Maybe when she was thirty...six...or something. After working a few years in her chosen field, building up a nice nest egg, maybe buying a house, she could consider an eligible male for companionship. Have a family. Or get a poodle. *Whatever.*

Lindsey stepped out of the dressing room wearing something that looked like it was ripped off the set of *Little House on the Prairie.*

What on earth? Stella smirked. "Is it a costume party, honey?"

Lindsey didn't laugh. Heck, she didn't even smile. In fact, her beaming expression faded to sunset pink. "I—I kind of like the old-style."

Stella strolled over to her daughter. She considered the flower-print, the long sleeves, long full skirt, tight bodice, high neckline, and frowned. The whole thing screamed "modest girl."

Lindsey stepped in front of the long mirror, smiled tremulously, and twirled. Her smile widened. A happy light beamed from her eyes.

Stella stepped back and considered the whole package. Gosh, the girl was stunning. She would be beautiful in a straight jacket.

Stella choked. Why had that image come to mind? Because Joanna was insane, living out her last years in a home for the mentally unbalanced? Lindsey was nothing like Joanna.

"Mom? You okay?"

"Yeah. Honey. Just wondering...what your dad will think. He's into the fashion model types."

Lindsey shook her head, perplexity and annoyance rippling in waves over her features. "You want me to dress like one of Dad's girlfriends?"

"No! Of course not." *So why did I say that?* Stella squared her shoulders. I just don't want you to hightail it to the other extreme. There's got to be something between bare all and cover all." She marched to the dress aisle and started shoving unworthies down the rack.

"But, Mom, I like this one. I like the flowers and the soft, comfortable texture. I don't want to expose my behind or my breasts or worry that some guy will think I'm looking for action. I like *me* in this one."

Stella swallowed. Hard. She dared not glance at her own plunging neckline or notice the fact that she could hardly cross her legs. *Everyone wears…*

Joanna's battered face, her scarred wrists. Puncture marks in her arms sobbed while her voice merely babbled incoherencies. *"Don't. Like. Me!"*

Stella refocused. "Your great-grandma would like it. Or maybe Uncle Peter."

The guy married at twenty-seven, had five kids, two adopted, and volunteered for some men's church organization. Had to give it to him, though. Never missed a family function, served at every funeral dinner, and could chat about sports till her ex dropped under the table. He was even nice enough to drive the slob home on occasion.

"So can I get it?" A mischievous grin sparkled in Lindsey's eyes. "You know, Great-grandma always said she'd watch over me. I think she'd tell you to let me get this dress."

The brown-skinned, wizened face and those startlingly beautiful blue eyes. The firm chin and no-nonsense demeanor. *Though she could outshine the sun when she smiled. She loved Joanna so. Nearly broke her heart…*

"Ma'am?"

Stella looked up.

The perfectly manicured clerk stood next to Lindsey. Concern scribbled all over her exhausted face. "Arc you all right?" She stepped closer, one arm out as if to offer a helping hand. "You want me to call your husband…or someone?"

Stella shook her head, tearing the cobwebs away. Heck no. She was fine. Her ex was across town probably gearing up for a night on the town.

"Checking out the old watering holes," he'd say. *And the women,* she knew.

She pulled her purse around to her front and unzipped the top, pulled out her wallet and wiggled her credit card from the proper pocket. "Here, we'll take it." She glanced at Lindsey's shocked but pleased expression. "You ought to be comfortable in your own clothes, honey." *And in your body. Your mind. Your soul...*

After they got in the car, Lindsey laid her new dress in the back seat. Then she reached over and hugged her mom.

Stella blinked back tears.

~~~

As Stella dressed for bed, she grabbed her usual black nightie, flung it on her body, and then stared at the long bathroom mirror. She wasn't a kid anymore. That much was obvious. But who was she? *Whose* was she?

A chime rang. She scurried to her bedside table and snatched up the phone.

Not a call. Just that stupid auto-reminder thing. Tomorrow's Joanna's birthday. Great-grandma used to bring a cake and balloons for everyone. Always wore those horrid old polyester pants and faded button-down blouses. But her grin as she hugged Joanna was the pot of gold at the end of the rainbow.

Stella tiptoed down the hall. A light shone under Lindsey's door. She knocked.

"Yeah?"

Stella opened the door and leaned in.
~~~

Lindsey sat in bed with her Kindle propped on her knees. She waited. Teen patience incarnate.

"Hey, honey. I was just thinking. How about you come with me to give Joanna a little birthday party tomorrow? We'll buy a cake and some of those wild balloons she used to like."

Straightening, Lindsey's face lit up. "I'd love to! I'll bring the family album. You know how she loves to see pictures of Great-grandma."

Stella paused and then leaped into the abyss. "Think we should invite your dad?"

Lindsey frowned. Confused.

"She is *his* sister, after all."

Lindsey tilted her head. "You know, I almost forgot that." She nodded. "Yeah. He should come." Her gaze wandered back to the page.

Satisfied, Stella blew her daughter a kiss. "Oh, and wear your new dress." Then she started back to her room, humming a tune... *Why wait for tomorrow?*

No Reasonable Cause

Originally published on The Writings of A. K. Frailey
1/17/2020

"What the hell just happened?" Joe knew his blood pressure had risen to dangerous heights, but there was no way he was going to back down. He had to have an explanation, even if there was no reasonable cause in sight.

"Well, sir…" The younger, slimmer man, somewhere in his twenties, rubbed his gloved hands together, probably attempting to maintain circulation in the biting January wind. He glanced up at the overpass. "It appears like some ice just flew off and smacked into your windshield."

Joe returned his gaze to his minivan packed to the brim with his family, an insanely hyperactive dog, and two miniature palm trees, his wife, in a spirit of well-I-can't-just-say-no-now-can-I? had accepted from her grieving sister, who was inundated with funeral plants after the untimely death of her husband in a railroad accident.

"I have a cousin who'll come out and fix that windshield in a jiffy. He's pretty close by, and his rates are reasonable."

A throb jumped from Joe's heart to his head. His wife looked like she had been turned to stone, and the dog, with his tongue hanging out, scrabbled at the back window like a deranged con artist trying to escape a long prison sentence.

Joe jogged forward, slid open the back door, and barked at his eldest son. "Cody, take him for a walk but don't go too far."

Slowly, one lanky jean-clad leg appeared, quickly followed by four shaggy doglegs and then the rest of the desperate hound. The complete boy followed in due course. The boy stood on the roadside wide-eyed but calm. The dog, wild-eyed, lunged against the restraints of the synthetic blue leash.

The boy swept his gaze up and down the busy highway and then stared at his dad. "Where?"

Joe pointed to the metal rail dividing the opposite lanes of traffic. "Walk along that, but stay close. Don't let Hunter go, or it'll be the end of him."

Joe ducked his head in through the open doorway and tapped the other two kids on their respective knees. "It'll be okay, guys. No problems."

His wife, Mary, sat stiff, facing forward, her shoulders rigid. The cracked windshield seemed to accent her solid form. He patted her shoulder and felt her collarbone. *When did she get so thin?* Joe spoke to the back of her head. "The guy outside said he knows someone who can fix the windshield, but it's only broken on your side. I can see well enough to make it home."

He wanted confirmation— "Yes, honey, that sounds good to me." —would have been music to his ears. But she didn't say anything. What? Like a big chunk of ice blowing off an overpass and smashing their windshield was his fault?

"It wasn't my fault, you know."

"We know, Dad." It was his middle kid, Taylor. She always took his part. Even when he didn't deserve it. Like the time he forgot the roast in the oven, and Mary came home to a smoke-filled house with a cinder block for dinner. Taylor had insisted that it was the roasting pan's fault.

Mary had tossed both the blackened pan and the burned dinner in the trash and made peanut butter jelly sandwiches with tomato soup for dinner.

Joe considered her now. She didn't need explanations, just the next step.

He, on the other hand, wanted to smack something. Or someone.

He turned to the skinny guy still rubbing his hands together, closed the car door, and stepped over. "Look, I think we'll be okay." He felt for his keys in his pocket and then remembered that they were still in the ignition. "It's not like the car is out of commission or anything. It just cracked the windshield. We'll make it home. I'll have our guy in town take care of it tomorrow."

The skinny guy seemed disappointed. He really wanted to help? Or did he get paid for referrals? Joe scratched his head. "I appreciate your stopping to check on us." He stuck out his hand.

Skinny guy glanced aside, blinked, and then clasped Joe's hand. "No problem. My sister was in a car accident last month. She and her husband. Dead. Newlyweds, too." He shrugged. "Some things can't be explained. But people can help. Sometimes." He bobbed his head and jogged back to his car. With a quick wave, he darted inside and drove off.

Hound and boy reentered the family minivan, and Joe, with a last surveying glance at the cracked windshield, threw himself into the driver's seat.

Relief flooded his system as the car rumbled to life. He glanced in the rearview mirror, offered a brave smile to his kids and the relieved hound, waited for an opening, and then merged into the late afternoon traffic. He ignored his wife.

As the last rays of the sun faded, and he made the turn onto the lane leading home, Mary's voice startled Joe out of his reverie. He glanced into the rearview mirror. The kids seemed to have fallen asleep. Even the dog was snoring.

"He was right."

Joe slackened the pressure on the gas pedal and let the car coast the last bit to their driveway. "How's that?"

"The guy who tried to help. He couldn't do anything. He couldn't explain why the ice fell on our car, why his sister was killed. Why Kelly's husband died."

Joe frowned. "He didn't even know—"

Mary turned and faced him. Speared him with her gaze more like. "I have a point here."

Joe knew perfectly well that he wasn't the sharpest blade in the cutlery drawer. His wife often sighed and merely shook her head when he missed some metaphysical point she was making. He needed to *try* to understand. He let the car come to a smooth stop in their driveway and squinted with intellectual concentration.

"You wanted to know what happened. Remember?"

"Yeah..."

"Well, we'll never know exactly how the ice came to hit our car. But we do know that some decent guy tried to help us."

Joe swallowed. "Yeah?"

"And perhaps that's enough."

For her, maybe. But he had every intention of starting an investigation of overpasses and the number of icicles that fell and hit passing cars. Still, if it worked for her... "If it makes you happy, honey."

She shook her head and smiled as she unbuckled. "You may figure out how to stop icicles from falling from overpasses...but you won't figure out why bad things happen."

Joe flipped his seat buckle off his shoulder and glanced back at his kids waking from sleep. He chewed his lip and then leaned over and spoke in a soft undertone. "No. But my job is to keep my family safe. And your job—" he stepped out and pulled open the back door, moving aside for the dog's explosion from the car.

Mary emerged from the passenger side and peered at her husband. Waiting.

"You make the best of the situation. No matter what."

The kids straggled to the house. A tired yawn escaped the youngest as she leaned on Taylor. Cody chased the dog to the backyard.

Myriads of stars twinkled from a black sky. The frozen air tingled Joe's fingers and nose. He exhaled a frosty breath as he met his wife in front of their minivan. He wrapped his arm around her waist. "You need to eat more. You're getting thin."

She snuggled into his shoulder. “I’ll make dinner tonight, and you can deal with the car—and underpasses—in the morning.”

Joe’s heart settled into a peaceful rhythm. “Makes sense to me, honey.”

To Be Content

Originally published on The Writings of A. K. Frailey
1/3/2020

Regina would rather face a mob of angry clowns than admit that she wasn't partial to puppies. After all, what kind of lunatic didn't like puppies? So, when her friend and (lucky for her brother) sister-in-law, Claudia, asked if she'd watch their puppy while they took a sneak trip to Chicago for a weekend of theater and dancing, who was Regina to say no?

"Suuure—" She tried to toss a happy exclamation mark into her voice, but it cracked at the crucial moment.

Claudia packed in such a hurry she wouldn't have missed a question mark streaking through the room buck-naked.

"Should I check in on him—her?—a couple of times a day?"

If Claudia had slammed her chest any harder, cardiac arrest would surely have ensued. "Oh, no! That won't do. Not at all. The Timster needs around-the-clock care. You'll take him to your place for the weekend. After all, he's our little baby!"

At that moment, said baby was snatched from happily chewing a pink slipper on the rumpled bed into mommy's arms. And rocked.

To its credit, the mutt had sense enough to look sheepish.

"Honey!"

Regina would know her brother's voice if he was a penguin returning from an iceberg in the frozen north. It was that distinctive. Rog didn't so much call as bellow. She honestly didn't understand it. No one else in the family bellowed. Must go back generations. She'd have to ask mom—without sending the woman into fits of *my-family-is-perfect* hysteria.

Rog's eyes lit up like a master criminal sizing up a safety deposit box. He even rubbed his hands together. "Hey, Regina! Glad you could make it! We'll head out before traffic gets crazy! Thanks for taking our little boy!"

Despite the contagion of exclamation points flung into the air, said *boy* was now transferred to daddy so mommy could slam her bag shut, snatch a faux fur coat off the chair, and toss a kiss in Regina's direction.

"You're a lifesaver, dear!"

Rog dumped his four-footed progeny into his sister's arms before skedaddling out the door.

Regina held the squirming puppy and wondered what it ate besides slippers.

~~~

Safely ensconced in her favorite chair, a novel on her right, a half-finished ghostwriting assignment on her left, a cup of hot cocoa warming her hands, she watched the puppy chase a ball of colored yarn across the floor. Regina decided that life—despite a twenty-minute I-will-be-calm-no matter-what-your-mother-says conversation with her dad—was pretty good. For her, at least.
~~~

A chime lifted her gaze from the miniature acrobat skidding into her coffee table to the green apartment door.

The rest of the apartment—painted Sahara tan—made the eye-catching door stand out like an oasis in the desert. *Maybe that was the point?* Dismissing the ever-present conundrum, Regina paced across the floor and peered through the peephole. "Yes?"

"It's me! Goofy. Let me in." Doing her signature cross-eyed, tongue-out look, Janet wiggled two fingers.

Regina smothered a sigh, considered hiding the puppy in her bedroom, imagined her computer cords chewed to frazzled ends, clutched the door handle and let her friend in. "Hey, Janet."

"Hey to you." Janet paraded into the room. The woman simply could not walk normally. Her hips swayed, her shoulders danced, her eyes romped. Sexy coolness personified.

Then she saw the puppy and melted into a puddle. "Ohhhh...a puuupppyyy!!!" She scooped the suddenly terror-stricken critter into her arms.

Fear soon gave way to annoyance. The Timster squirmed like a child on a dentist's chair.

"When did you get a puppy? Why didn't you tell me? I thought I was your best friend—"

"It's my brother's and his wife's. I'm baby—I mean—dog-sitting for the weekend. Don't tell anyone. I'm not sure how my landlady would react since she enforces a No Pets law throughout the kingdom."

Janet smirked. "Couldn't get a date with a guy, huh?"

Regina dangled colored yarn in front of the frolicking mutt, making them both dance.

In an attempt to regain some measure of dignity, the puppy snatched the yarn and ran to the kitchen.

Regina returned to her chair and retrieved her cocoa from the end table. “I’m off the online sites, and I have no plans.”

If prohibition had made a comeback, Janet couldn’t have looked more horrified. “What happened? I thought you liked some of the guys.”

“Liking and making a life together are two different things.”

“So, what do you want?”

“A friend first. Then we’ll see.”

“But you already got me.” Janet started for the kitchen. “Well, Tuesday through Thursday.”

Regina drained her cup and followed the swaying hips. “So, what are you doing here? It’s Friday. You should be out on the town with…”

“Yeah. I’m going. I just wanted to ask you something first.”

Regina set the cup on the kitchen counter, faced her friend, and raised her eyebrows

“Gerry asked me to marry him.”

Regina’s heart flipped. *Jealous? Nope. Well, maybe. A little.* “Yeah? So…?”

“Should I say yes?”

Thc puppy sauntered across the tiled floor, head up, chest out, clutching the skein of yarn in his teeth like a wolf carrying venison home to the pack.

Regina lifted her gaze to the older woman, and for the first time, she really looked. And saw. The too-bright lipstick, the heavy makeup, faint shadows under her eyes, the long-suffering expression.

"What do *you* want, Janet?"

Janet shook her head. "I want what you got. With puppy. And your books. Work. Your bellowing brother, your persnickety mom and worn-out dad. Your damn—contentment."

Regina laughed. It felt good to laugh. At her friend. At herself. At the silly puppy. "Goofy indeed, you are rightly named! Tell me, do you enjoy getting hungry?"

Janet turned her head, glaring from one eye. "Generally, before meals."

"So being fed all the time wouldn't suit you any more than being content all the time. You just haven't learned to be content with periodic—"

"Discontent?"

"Yeah."

"Well, Gerry's not perfect, but he loves me, and I—" The hips relaxed, her shoulders settled, and her eyes softened. "I rather like the guy."

"Can you make a life with him?"

"We can try. If there's a will—right?" She looked down as the doggy trotted near. "But what about you—and your temporary little friend?"

The Timster dropped the defeated yarn at Regina's feet and peered up adoringly.

Regina scooped the puppy into her arms and chuckled all the way back to her chair.

Your Prayer

Originally published on The Writings of A. K. Frailey
12/20/2019

Kelog chewed his lip as he watched an oversized gnat circle the room. Why didn't someone smash the blinking thing into oblivion? He would. Certainly. If it got close enough. But it never did. Fury seethed through his whole system. Gnats shouldn't be flying about on a frozen December day. They had no right to exist. Not here. Not now.

A gale wind struck the windowpane. *Dang! Driving home will be hell. Not as bad as the drive here, though. That's not possible.* He wiped sweat from his hands, rubbing them along his jeans. He glared at the fake poinsettia, the cheery signs on the wall with comforting platitudes, the assembly of gray humanity sitting hunched over their phones on lounge chairs that no one ever lounged on. Kelog loathed waiting rooms.

He peered at the doorway. He wanted to be in *there*. With his wife. But given the fact that he had carried her into the emergency room screaming for help, medics had promptly laid her on a stretcher and then—in no uncertain terms—ushered him out, he figured he shouldn't distract them from their primary concern. Laurie. And the baby.

How could such a wonderful day have gone so wrong?

They had snuggled in bed, comforting each other. Calm. Loving. The gray skies only highlighted the red and green decorations hanging in ornamental beauty along the porch railing. Quickly dressed. A strong cup of coffee. A kiss goodbye that hinted of pleasures intended for after work hours.

The day had flown by. “Any day now…” everyone had chanted with twinkles in their hope-filled eyes. And they weren’t talking about Santa and a new train set.

He had come home early. A surprise. He knew how tired Laurie had been, and he wanted to help clean the house before the big family gathering. She had probably done most of it, he knew. But in her condition, she never got as much done as she intended. And he was going to be her knight in shining armor and come to the rescue. He even brought home a new mop!

But after a twenty-minute drive against a roaring wind, parking in the snug garage, whistling his way into the kitchen armed with his playful sword-mop, he glanced around.

Somewhere in the universe, a sorceress plucked a low, vibrating chord. An oddity jumped at him from the corner of his eye. His morning coffee cup sat unwashed in the sink. Perplexity somersaulted right into anxiety.

“Laurie?” He laid the mop with a bow wrapped around it on the kitchen table where she couldn’t miss it. “Hey, honey! Guess what?”

Silence swept over his arms and chilled his bones.

“Laurie?”

He could hear his own footsteps as he pounded upstairs two at a time to their bedroom. Horrible images filled his mind. And then his heart.

She lay in bed, still as stone. Cold to his touch.

Calling for an ambulance never crossed his mind. The hospital was down the street, and his car was warm and close. Without conscious thought, he bundled her into his arms, her snoopy pajamas flaring and her arms flopping to the sides, and he trotted downstairs with the two most precious people in the universe.

"Mr. Jones?"

Kelog peered up. The gnat swirled in the air before him. He stood.

"The doctor will be here in a moment. Have you called anyone?"

Kelog blinked. His mouth dropped open. He knew he looked stupid. He felt stupid. Not idiotic, just unable to think. Unable to process her words. "Call? Who?"

The nurse pressed his arm, gesturing back to the chair. As if sitting might help him think. "Your family? Her family? Parents?"

Yes. Of course. He should call someone. But who? And say what? He glanced at the nurse. Her uniform tag said "Beatrice."

Nothing mattered. Except his wife. And the baby. "How are they?"

Beatrice had perfected the non-committal smile. "I really can't say too much. The doctor will be here in a moment. I just came to check on you and see if you want me to call anyone. If you need anything?"

An award-winning android could not have moved more precisely. Kelog pulled his phone from his shirt pocket, hit the contacts list, pointed to Nestly Smith, and cleared his throat. "My sister. She'll know what to do."

With a compliant nod, Beatrice rose, tapped the phone and put it to her ear. She strolled a few feet away, stopping in front of a crucifix hanging on the wall.

Kelog blinked. *I should be praying. I should've called mom. I should have...done something.*

But nothing mattered. Time had stopped when that dark chord had struck. Life had ceased to exist as he knew it. Was he even breathing?

"Sir?"

Beatrice held out the phone. "She wants to talk to you."

Kelog pressed the phone to his ear.

"I'm coming. Tom's getting the car, and we'll be there in about twenty minutes. Hang on, sweetheart. She'll be okay. Everything will be all right."

Tears flooded Kelog's eyes. A million gnats swarmed around him. "But I didn't call an ambulance. I forgot to pray. Never thought to call Mom..."

"I'll call Mom. We'll all be there. Soon. Hang on! Don't give up."

"She was cold. Really cold, Nes."

"I'm praying, Kelly. Tom's praying. Everyone who knows us will be praying."

"I even brought home a mop."

Kelog felt the shadow stop before him. The phone slipped from his fingers. He stood and faced the doctor.

"Mr. Smith, your wife had slipped into a coma—but she's recovering now."

Kelog heard himself whisper. "The baby?"

"She's fine. Probably didn't notice a thing. Just thought her mama was resting all day. Which, in a way, she was. Diabetic shock. It could've been worse. But she came out of it, and they'll both be fine. We'll just have to keep a close eye on them."

The rest of the doctor's words blurred as Beatrice, with a surprisingly firm grip, directed him to his wife's bedside.

Laurie's pale face broke into a sheepish grin when their eyes met. "I didn't follow the doc's directions last night…you know…I had other things on my mind."

"Oh, God. I thought I'd lost you."

Beatrice and the doctor meandered to the far side of the room.

Laurie's grin widened. "You can't lose me, love. Your prayers probably saved me."

The gnat darted in front of Kelog's eyes. He slammed his hands together, making everyone jump. When he spread his hands wide, a black smear decorated his palms. "Damn bug." He glanced at his wife. "It distracted me; I forgot—"

A lightning bolt of sisterly anxiety sped into the room and catapulted into her brother's arms. "I got here as soon—" She glanced over to the bed and shrieked. "You're okay!" Veering from brother to sister-in-law, Nestly flung herself into Laurie's arms.

Tom sauntered up and pressed Kelog's shoulder. No words needed.

~~~
~~~

An hour later, after a fast-food run, Kelog stepped through the waiting room with two paper bags loaded with a selection that would've sent his high school health teacher into a panic attack.

Beatrice stood before the crucifix. Staring.

His mood leaping amid moonbeams, Kelog hardly missed a beat as he changed his trajectory and stopped beside the middle-aged woman. "Thank you. For today. For thinking of me and calling my sister."

Beatrice looked over. She wiped away an errant tear. "I was glad to help."

Kelog pointed to the cross and shrugged, unable to comprehend his lapse. "I forgot to pray."

Beatrice shook her head. "No. You didn't. Your love is your prayer. I only wish everyone prayed as much."

And to Think

Originally published on The Writings of A. K. Frailey
10/10/2019

Stacy stared at the enrollment form and frowned at the first line. She hated her name. No imagination at all. Her parents might just as well have named her munchkin or kiddo.

Perched on the edge of an icy blue cafeteria chair, she sipped from a steaming cup of mud-colored cocoa. She had taken the entire afternoon off from work just so she could sign up for a night class that would inch her one step closer to getting her teaching degree. Not that she wasn't already teaching. But only as an assistant. If she wanted the title and pay of a "real" teacher, she needed the certificate with her name on it.

Youngsters looking very much like loping trees bustled down the corridor, talking, shoving, laughing in the way that carefree youth usually do. Conflicts with the landlord, insurance issues, and a steamy romance gone haywire probably didn't disturb their optimistic lives. Her mom, a couple of good friends, and a decent job didn't a thrilling life make. She wished she were someone else with a better name. She tapped her purple pen, inscribed with a goofy cartoon character down one side, against her mini-notepad. Nothing new to write today.

She took another sip of cocoa, closed her eyes, and sighed.

Two chairs scraped on her right and an on-going conversation dominated the swirling sounds around her. Two trays plunked down on the table, plastic smacking plastic. A woman's voice—excited, eager, and determined clawed at Stacy's insides.

Don't listen! Keep your mind on the cocoa! She popped her eyes open, clutched the cup like a drowning victim gripping a lifeline and swallowed a burning gulp.

The woman rattled on mercilessly. "And so—I told my husband, 'You're so ignorant, and then I slammed the door in his face.'"

Stacy wondered if it would look odd if she pressed her hands against her ears and started rocking in place.

The other woman's voice piped up, practically breathless. "And then?"

Stacy stared at her pen, focusing on the inane figure. A student had presented this gift as a token of her appreciation for Stacy's effort to teach her long division using pictures and creative stories. She knew the child would probably be haunted by math for the rest of her life, but apparently, the kid appreciated sincere efforts. Stacy glanced aside, hoping the two women had evaporated.

The first woman clearly liked bright flowers, for she wore an eye-catching blouse that would have put a landscape artist to shame. But unfortunately, her language was as loud as her clothes. "So, the idiot slept on the couch!"

A psychic warrior battling for peace of mind—jabbing at judgments, parrying insinuations, knocking off observations, and blasting conclusions could not have fought any harder. But nevertheless, a picture of a man's sad, pathetic face as the door closed on him...and then his drooping figure trudging to a sagging couch and flopping down in a bundle of husbandry despair filled Stacy with red-eyed rage.

A little voice tried to reason with her. *You don't know these people, woman!*

She whirled her gaze around the food court. Uncaring neon signs glared back: Asian Delights, Mexican Combos, All American Platters, and a Salad Bar.

Inhale. Exhale. *Mind your own business!*

Stacy slurped her cold cocoa and then mopped up the dribbles dotting the table.

The lively chatting continued though the voices dropped an octave.

New pictures formed in Stacy's mind. A shoe sale, something about church services, and a trip to the airport with a secret admirer?

Enough! Stacy jumped to her feet, wondering if it was possible to have her imagination disconnected from her brain. She dumped her Styrofoam cup into the trashcan and headed for the door.

Once out in the late afternoon sunshine, she prompted her feet toward the football-field-sized parking lot. Her car was out there...somewhere.

A child's scream turned her attention. With a hand blocking the slanting rays of the sun, she scanned the area. There, next to a table and bench on a grassy field, stood a lanky man wearing jeans and a black hoodie, gripping the arm of a young girl in a pink skirt and an oversized sweater. The child struggled to pull away.

Stacy's heart constricted. She fumbled for her phone, but as her panic increased, she hustled toward the child faster than her fingers could unzip her purse. She halted before the pair, staring or glaring, she wasn't sure.

The child glanced at Stacy, cut the scream dead, and slammed herself against the man, wrapping her arms around his middle and pressing her face into his stomach.

A burning blush tingled from Stacy's face to the roots of her hair. She scratched her head and wavered.

The man waved as if conducting an orchestra. "She's being dramatic. Like always, eh, honey bun?" He peered down at the child, and a grin played on his lips. "Not too happy that Mama is taking a class, and you can't be in on the action?"

"Oh." Stacy hadn't a clue what else to say.

The girl pulled away, propped her hands on her hips, tilted her head, and accused Stacy. "You're a teacher here!"

Stacy lifted her hands in surrender. "Oh, no, ma'am. I do help out at school, and I want to be a teacher someday. But right now, I'm just taking classes, like your mom."

The child nodded in defeat. She leaned comfortably against the man. "Daddy? Can't I at least draw something? It's so boring out here."

Now it was the man's turn to flush. "Sorry, baby. I left your pencils at home."

Stacy plunged her hand into her purse and pulled out her notepad and purple pen. "Here, kiddo, take these. You can draw pictures for your mama and give them to her when she comes out. I bet she'll like that."

The man tried to wave off the gifts, but the child took them with eager hands and a surprisingly charming grin.

Once she found her car and started the long drive home, Stacy glanced in the mirror and laughed. “Who’s the kiddo, eh?”

That's How It Goes

Originally published on The Writings of A. K. Frailey
6/27/2019

"God, how I love my life." The sun was shining, birds were singing, and the green park, with purple and pink flowerbeds, brown benches, and scurrying squirrels, looked as gorgeous as any storybook garden. "So why is my heart so torn and ragged?"

The college buildings rose up before Victoria's eyes, a U-shaped arrangement of stone structures built in imitation of the grand European universities. A tower with a clock set inside a green cupola bore testimony to stronger eyes. She couldn't see the hands, much less the numbers. But it didn't matter. Her son's campus tour would take three hours, so she had plenty of time before the long trek back home.

Home?

Out of five kids, Thomas was the youngest. And now it was his turn to spread his wings and fly away. The older four had fulfilled their destiny—college, good jobs, and two were married now. The second child, the only girl, had had a baby last winter.

Victoria was happy for them. She was thrilled that Thomas had found a college that he really liked and was eager to start classes in the fall. Everything was terrific. Wonderful. Blessed.

So why did an aching depression choke her soul?

A white minivan pulled into the parking lot, and three kids tumbled out. A toddler scampered forward into the arms of a young woman...a big sister? Victoria's heart clenched. The father, thirtyish with graying temples, and the mother, wearing a long summer dress, joined the clutch around the young woman. Hugs and hellos and comments mixed together into a bright cacophony of delight.

Victoria felt the tear before she realized she was crying. Why on earth was she upset? Couldn't she be happy for this family reunion? Even though it wasn't hers...and never would be again?

Terry had passed away four years ago. Despite the agony of loss, she had shouldered her responsibilities and raised the kids as they had always planned. And the kids had surpassed their parents' every hope and dream.

But she had never looked any further...to a life beyond the kids. Beyond marriage. Beyond her responsibilities. Once Thomas moved into the dorm and out of the house, he would live his own life. Have meals with friends instead of with her. Do his own laundry. Well, most of the time. And have fun elsewhere.

Would home be home anymore?

Certainly, there would be get-togethers. Family dinners. Holidays. But her heart sank at the thought of it all. How her eldest wanted to spend last Christmas with his wife's family. Of course, it was her turn. And the grandbaby—grandbabies eventually—would have to be shared as well. She couldn't very well snatch the little ones and relive her happy motherhood.

No. She couldn't, really.

The happy family moved off toward the main entrance, a celebratory look on all their faces, except for one. A teen girl. She moped. In a bad mood probably. Victoria wanted to grab the child and shake her, get into her face and make her listen. *You've only got a little time. Don't waste it! Don't ruin the day for the others. Life is so damn short.*

The father took the teen under his wing as they went through the doorway, and the child peered up with adoring eyes. The father glanced away, a cloud passing over his face. He knew. A shadow loomed.

But distant laughter broke the spell, the door shut, and Victoria was left with the birds. She reached into her bag and pulled out a novel. Some mystery or another. Anything to distract her thoughts. To make the hours pass so she could go home again and live...just a while longer...

An old woman toddled near, hobbling with the aid of a cane. She stopped when she saw Victoria.

Matching benches stood across from each other. Victoria looked over. A large splotch of bird poop marred the other one. She grimaced and scooted aside. There was room, after all.

The woman nodded in gratitude and inched her way near.

Victoria stood and helped her sit, suddenly terrified that the frail body would slip and break a bone, and she'd have to call 9-1-1 and...

Once settled, the lady chuckled. "I used to be a long-distance runner. Never guess it now."

Victoria eyed the spare figure with new appreciation. "Really? How wonderful! I mean, that must've been very exciting."

"Ronda the Runner...that was my name. I was something of a star here...long years ago. There have all my trophies in their wall cabinet, awards and such. I donated them when I sold my house. No point in keeping them. I know what I did. Memories are glorious...for a while. Then it's time to let go."

A sigh erupted from Victoria's aching heart. She gazed at the flowers. A sudden image of ice and snow—the park covered in frozen death—enveloped her imagination. She heard her voice before she realized she had spoken. "And go where?"

Rhonda turned, her gaze sweeping over Victoria like a buyer at an auction. "Wherever life takes you. If you're still above ground...make the best of it."

"But when your heart hurts like it is being ripped in two? What then? When your old life is over and you have no new life to start?"

Rhonda waved a wrinkled hand and peered into the distance. "I remember...the day my sister was killed in a car crash. We were twins. It was like my body had burned with hers in the flames." She peered at her hands. "When I looked in the mirror, I saw a living being...but vacant eyes. Like I had died with her." With a grunt, Rhonda straightened. "But it was a lie. I wasn't dead. Rita was dead. I had to discover how to make a new life. Grow a new identity without my twin."

Tears flooded Victoria's eyes, and an ache swelled in her throat. She couldn't have spoken if the Queen of England implored her to.

A bell tolled three times. Another half hour and Thomas would be ready to leave.

Rhonda patted Victoria's knee. "Lost everyone...or just someone special?"

“Everyone special, just one at a time.

“That’s how it goes…if you live long enough.”

“I’d rather not.”

“Not your choice. You could try to cheat. But that’d just pass things along down the road. You’re going to face loss and misunderstanding and death…in a million forms before the end.” She chuckled. “You know what they used to say to me during the long practice runs when my whole body ached? ‘No pain, no gain.’” She waved away a passing insect. “Stupid phrase. It isn’t the pain that teaches you…it’s knowing that it won’t last…that it’s just a part of something bigger. Something better. I never expected to win anything. Not after Rita’s death. But I did. I won medal after medal. I learned I could still love my sister…even when I couldn’t see her or feel her. I endured. And now my great-grandson is starting his career as a runner. Wonderful boy. I’m happy for him.”

“So you married…and had a family…and they moved on… And your husband?”

“Cancer got him fifteen years ago.”

Victoria stared at the ground.

A sparrow flittered on the grass before them, hopping about, as if doing a happy dance.

Rhonda shrugged. “Well, I best start back now…it’ll take me a while to get to the reception area. They’re having a little party for him.” She wavered to her feet.

Victoria stood and reached out. “You want a hand? I can walk back with you. It’ll be time to pick up my son soon.”

"If you'd like. We can share the path before we go our separate ways. Got to be glad for these little things."

At the doorway, Thomas waved at his mother.

Victoria let go of Rhonda's hand and watched the old woman unceremoniously disappear into a bright interior.

Thomas grinned. "Helping old ladies, Mom?"

Victoria took her son's arm, the dull ache settling into calm acceptance. "The other way around, more like." She wanted to tell him—"Don't laugh, my boy. It'll be your turn, soon enough." But that would be cruel. Now was his time to smile and be glad.

A fresh wave of love comforted her soul. She was happy for him.

A. K. Frailey

A. K. Frailey has written the historical sci-fi *OldEarth Encounter* series, a contemporary first contact novel, *Last of Her Kind*, the *Newearth* sci-fi series, an *OldTown* series, short story collections, a modern parent's reflection on J. R. R. Tolkien's works in *The Road Goes Ever On: A Christian Journey Through The Lord of the Rings*, personal and introspective *My Road* books, children's books, and a poetry collection.

She taught elementary education in Milwaukee, WI; Chicago, IL; Los Angeles, CA; and Wood River, IL.

She also trained teachers in the Philippines for the Peace Corps and later earned a Master of Fine Arts Degree in Creative Writing for Entertainment from Full Sail University.

Ann homeschooled all her children and currently manages her rural homestead with her family and their numerous critters. In her spare time, she serves as an election judge and secretary/treasurer of her small town's cemetery.

A. K. Frailey Books QR CODES

A. K. Frailey Website

Translated Books Page with Links

A. K. Frailey Interviews Page

A. K. Frailey Amazon Author Page

www.ingramcontent.com/pod-product-compliance
Lightning Source LLC
Chambersburg PA
CBHW060625310726
48982CB00003B/682

9798987404751